# THE FAITHLESS HEART

*Betrayed by one she thought she could trust?*

Orphan Catriona Dunbar leaves her grandmother's Scottish village home to pay a visit to her father's cousins, the Espleys, at their home, Pelham. On hearing of her grandmother's death, Samuel Espley insists that he is now Catriona's guardian and forbids her to leave Pelham. She has befriended the mysterious hired help, Morgan Chappel, but he is jailed following allegations of wrecking and smuggling. Catriona must find out the truth about the shipwreck that killed her parents, if she is to prove Morgan's innocence, and avoid a forced marriage to Sir Julian Espley.

# The Faithless Heart

*by*

June Davies

**Dales Large Print Books**
Long Preston, North Yorkshire,
BD23 4ND, England.

British Library Cataloguing in Publication Data.

Davies, June
    The faithless heart.

A catalogue record of this book is
available from the British Library

ISBN   978-1-84262-663-4 pbk

38917413

First published in Great Britain 1994
by D. C. Thomson & Co. Ltd.

Copyright © June Davies 1994

Cover illustration by arrangement with P. W. A. International

The moral right of the author has been asserted

Published in Large Print 2008 by arrangement with
June Davies

Dales Large Print is an imprint of Library Magna Books Ltd.

Printed and bound in Great Britain by
T.J. (International) Ltd., Cornwall, PL28 8RW

# CHAPTER ONE

Catriona Dunbar stood before her window at Pelham, tying the frayed ribbons of her camisole as she stared down across the wet gardens and beyond the weathered gate to the shore fields with their tall, coarse grasses and clumps of hardy sea hollies.

The tide was ebbing, the power of its great crashing waves spent as it receded, flat and grey and pin-cushioned with fine needles of November rain. A brigantine with furled sails bound for Liverpool was blurry on the distant horizon, almost like a ghost ship.

Almost like the Rhiannon, Catriona realised.

Catriona had been a little girl, plucked from the churning sea and dragged aboard a row-boat by rescuers who had put out from Friars Quay, but her parents' lives had been among the many lost that stormy, spring night.

It all seemed so very long ago, and yet...

From the corner of her eye, Catriona glimpsed the paleness of her wedding gown, laid across the high, narrow, brass bed. She shivered. The past often haunted her now.

Catriona's hazel eyes darkened with despair – whom had she to blame but herself?

The bedroom door swung open and a young maidservant wearing a faded dress covered by a voluminous, patched apron entered briskly.

'Mr Julian's nearly finished breakfast, and he said why haven't you come down?'

'Not this morning, Eliza.'

The maid nodded, taking Catriona's stays and petticoats from the dresser drawer. 'Thought not, ma'am. It's bad luck to see the bridegroom on the day of the wedding – I told the master that, but he wouldn't listen. Just roared with laughter and said I was spouting nonsense.'

Catriona stepped into the petticoats that Eliza held, standing quite still as the maid fastened the ties.

It was indeed a wry quirk of fate which had thrown the two women together this way. After the suspicions and jealousies that had once existed between them, Eliza was the nearest to a friend that Catriona had left in the world.

A quick knot of tension tightened inside Catriona. By the day's end, this room would no longer be hers. After the marriage ceremony that evening, she'd be expected to share the master bedroom with Julian Espley.

'There, ma'am!' Eliza said, smoothing down the layers of petticoats with her work-reddened hands. 'Got the tiniest waist in the whole county, I reckon! You'll look a right treat in your wedding dress. Mr Julian's a lucky man, I reckon.'

Catriona heard the catch in the maid's voice, and looked around quickly. Eliza at once turned away, but not before Catriona had glimpsed the pensive expression in her eyes.

'Eliza...?' Catriona began awkwardly.

'Don't, ma'am.' The maid's face was drawn and sallow in the dull light cast by the candles. 'Don't pity me. I can't bear it. 'Sides, it's not the wedding– Well, not only that, anyhow.'

'Then what?' Catriona persisted gently, impulsively closing her own small hand about Eliza's larger, rough one.

Eliza chewed the inside of her cheek anxiously. 'He's back, ma'am!' she blurted at last. 'I wasn't sure whether to say nothing – but he's back!'

'Morgan...' The name fell as a whisper from Catriona's lips as she stared in dis-

7

belief at Eliza. She felt the colour draining from her face. Her legs were suddenly too weak to support her weight, and Catriona gripped the carved bedpost, sinking down heavily on to the corner of the mattress.

'Where is he?'

'I saw him down on the shore, ma'am,' Eliza said.

'If he's caught here in Friars Quay, he'll hang, Eliza!' Catriona almost choked on the words.

'After so long I thought – prayed – Morgan would have left the country.' She turned questioning eyes on Eliza. 'Whatever can have brought him back?'

'Only one reason there can be, I reckon,' Eliza commented. 'Your wedding.'

'Did you talk to him, Eliza?' Catriona's heart was pounding.

The maid gave her an incredulous look. 'I surely did not! Morgan didn't even see me, ma'am! I made certain of that!'

Catriona could understand that Eliza might be shocked, dismayed even, by Morgan's return – however, she was mystified by the peculiar emotion she read in the other girl's face.

'Eliza, you're afraid!' she murmured. 'But why? Morgan would never hurt you. What

8

reason would he have? If anyone has reason to fear Morgan,' Catriona went on in a low voice, 'it is I. After all, it was my word that sent Morgan to prison. That he is now an escaped convict who must always hide and run, is my doing.'

'Aye, but we don't–' Eliza broke off in alarm, and Catriona's senses lurched at the heavy footsteps bearing down along the landing.

'Eliza! Where are you, girl?'

'It's only Julian!' Catriona's sigh of relief was clearly audible.

In the next instant, Julian Espley's fist was pounding at Catriona's door.

'I thought I'd find you in here gossiping!' Julian's impatience was directed at Eliza. 'I'm already late. Where are my boots?'

Eliza glowered at him. 'I put them out for you, sir. After I'd cleaned them.'

'Well, I can't find them! Go and get them for me.'

The maid left the room to do as she was ordered.

'I've urgent business in Liverpool, but I shall return in good time for the ceremony.' Then, with a wicked grin, Julian left Catriona to her thoughts.

When Catriona was alone once more, she

returned to the window.

Her knuckles whitened as she gripped the ledge of the lattice-paned window, not wishing to recall the very last occasion she had seen Morgan – crouching dirty and ragged and humiliated in the vile filth of a crowded prison cell.

Other memories swam before her alone. Sharply vivid pictures of the day, almost three years ago, when she had discovered she was to visit Pelham.

## CHAPTER TWO

Brilliant sunlight reflecting from fresh-fallen snow filtered through the coloured, glass windows of the mossy, stone kirk in the Highlands' village of Strathlachie, shining down upon the faces of the small choir.

Oliver Stuart abruptly raised his bony hands from the keys of the organ and snapped his shrewd eyes on to the two rows of singers.

'No, no, no!' he said tersely.

Now Mr Stuart's stern gaze raked the back row of male voices, lingering purposefully upon the earnest, rather pale features of Gilbert Pierce. Sensing the scrutiny, Gilbert shuffled uncomfortably, lowering his eyes as he felt his smooth cheeks burning.

'Let's try again, choir,' Mr Stuart instructed, adding sharply. 'And softly, this time. Softly!'

The instant the choirmaster's attention was focussed upon his playing, Gilbert Pierce cautiously leaned forward to the row of women and girl singers and gently tugged one of Catriona Dunbar's glossy, blonde braids.

Fifteen-year-old Catriona started, raising her hazel eyes from her hymn book, but not daring to look around. She felt a slight tug upon her braid once again, and then a small, folded square of thick paper was tossed over her right shoulder, landing with a clumsy bounce on to the open pages of her book.

Catriona stifled a gasp of surprise, her eyes now fixed upon the choirmaster's back as she endeavoured to slide the paper from her book and into the safety of her palm without it rustling or being seen by keen-eyed Mr Stuart.

Sophy Hamilton elbowed Catriona in the ribs, and mouthed, 'Well done!' when Catriona chanced to glance sidelong at her

11

best friend.

'It was just so funny! – I thought I was going to burst!' Sophy exploded once practice was over and the girls were fetching their coats. 'When Gil's note bounced that way – oh, my! I thought it was surely going to bounce right down and hit Mr Stuart on his bald pate!'

She lowered her voice confidentially. 'What does Gil's note say?'

'I haven't read it yet,' Catriona answered, as they started out for the kirk. 'I'll open it–'

'Miss Dunbar!'

Catriona turned around, pausing on the kirk's worn, stone steps as the choirmaster hurried after her, wrapping a muffler about his long neck.

'Miss Dunbar, I wanted to ask after your grandmother? Is she feeling better?'

'Very much, thank you, Mr Stuart.' Catriona smiled. Essie McPherson had been poorly but was at last on the mend.

'Doctor Milne sees Granny every day, but he's pleased with her recovery.'

'You might tell Essie that I'll be sure to come by for a visit.' The choirmaster raised his hat and started away through the deep, frosty snow towards the manse. 'Cheer her up a wee bit.'

Sophy grimaced, leaning close to Catriona's ear. 'If I was feeling sick, a visit from vinegary, old Oliver Stuart would see me off altogether!'

'He's only being kind, Sophy,' Catriona said mildly.

The girls had been firm friends ever since Catriona came to Strathlachie as a wee girl to live with Grandmother McPherson. And despite their characters being as different as chalk from cheese, Catriona loved Sophy more dearly than any true sister might.

'What are you going to wear for the Social on Saturday night?' Sophy asked, adding gloomily, 'I'm having to make-over that blue serge I wore last winter! Oh, Catie! Don't you just long for wonderful, new dresses? Don't you wish you didn't have to wait until you're twenty-one to get your inheritance? I know I should!'

'I never think much about my inheritance,' Catriona replied truthfully. Her late father Alexander Dunbar had been a partner in a prosperous Liverpool firm of sugar refiners, and he and his wife had spent much of their married life overseas.

'To have some of the money would be very useful, of course,' Catriona went on seriously, pushing at the powdery snow with the snub

13

toe of her boot. 'There are comforts I should like to give Granny that we simply can't afford – but there really isn't anything else I'd want to buy.'

'You haven't any imagination!' Sophy chided brightly. 'Now, when are you going to open Gil's note? I'm dying to know what it says.' She peered around her friend's arm as Catriona began unfolding the thick paper.

'Oh, Catie!' Sophy cried, 'What does Gil say?'

'He wants me to meet him at the hollow log–'

Even as Catriona spoke, Sophy was holding on to her bonnet with one hand and using the other to raise her skirts clear of the snow.

Catriona got to the hollow log first. Gilbert was already there, waiting for her. He heard her approaching and looked around, calling out and smiling broadly as he ran to meet her.

However, Gilbert's callow face revealed dismay when he saw that Sophy Hamilton was following some three or four yards behind Catriona.

'Hello, Catriona,' he murmured. 'I'm glad you came–'

'You win, Catie!' Sophy panted, limping up to them, clutching her side. 'I'd have given you a closer race but for this wretched stitch!'

'Hello, Sophy,' Gilbert said absently, unable to take his eyes from Catriona's heart-shaped, pretty face. Her cheeks were rosy from the snowy afternoon and running, her eyes shining as she smiled up at him.

'I thought we might go skating. I brought my own skates.' Gilbert withdrew a mackintosh-wrapped bundle from within the hollow log. 'And I went to your grandmother's cottage and asked if I might have your skates, too. Annie fetched them for me.'

'What about mine?' Sophy exclaimed in dismay. 'How am I to skate?'

Gilbert flushed awkwardly. 'I'm sorry, Sophy. I just didn't think. If I'd realised you'd be here, too, I would've brought yours also, of course.'

'Never mind,' Catriona said at once, turning to Sophy. 'We wear the same size. We can share my boots and take turns at skating.'

'Thanks, you're a plum!' Sophy beamed. 'You go first. I'll rest and catch my breath for a minute, while this stitch in my side goes.'

While the girls sat on the log, Gilbert laced the heavy, brown, skating boots on to Catriona's slender feet, before bashfully taking her gloved hand into his own and leading her on to the ice. Then slowly drawing her away from Sophy's sight around the curving bank of the loch, Gilbert impulsively slipped his arms about Catriona's slim waist, lowering his lips to hers.

'Gilbert!' Catriona breathed, turning away. 'Don't—'

'Please, Catriona!' he mumbled thickly.

Catriona's pulse was suddenly racing as she felt the warmth of Gilbert's breath against her cheek, his mouth so urgently seeking hers, but she pushed him gently away from her.

Even as she slid from Gilbert's arms, skimming away across the shimmering loch, Catriona's senses soared with the sweet, heady emotions his touch had awakened within her.

Annie was just bustling down the garden path as Catriona turned into the gate with its trellised arch of evergreens.

'You're just in time, Miss Catriona!' Annie greeted her cheerfully. 'I've left tea laid and ready, all you've to do is warm the pot!'

'Thank you, Annie.' Catriona smiled gratefully at the housekeeper, who'd been a treasure during Essie McPherson's illness. 'How's Granny?'

'Oh, she's no' so bad.' Annie nodded.

'Even a bit perkier, I'd say. She received a letter after you'd left for choir practice, so perhaps that has something to do with it...'

Essie McPherson was sitting in her rocking chair beside the fire in the snug, low-beamed parlour. She smiled up as Catriona scurried indoors.

'Hurry and take off your things and come here. We'll have tea in front of the fire.' She patted the plump cushion beside her chair. 'I've some thrilling news for you...'

'Invited to Pelham?' Catriona exclaimed in astonishment some few minutes later when she was pouring the tea. 'I don't understand. We haven't heard from the Espleys in years!'

'Steady on, you'll have the tray over!' Essie laughed. 'However, you're quite correct. We did lose touch with them, which was quite wrong because the Espleys are your only other relatives and family is family, when all's said and done.

'But there, that's all put to rights now because Samuel Espley – your father's cousin – has written inviting you to spend the whole season at Pelham!'

'A trip – all the way to Friars Quay – to Lancashire!' Catriona shook her head in disbelief, sitting back on her heels. 'I've never been on a trip before!'

'Then it's high time you did, pet!' Essie said. 'You should get to know your cousins. Lucy, she's only a little older than you, and Julian, who must be about twenty-six by now. Perhaps he's even married with a family of his own.

'To be truthful,' she went on, 'I never did care much for Samuel Espley, and your father wasn't close to him either. But they were cousins, and family meant a great deal to Alex.'

'What's Samuel like?' Catriona asked, curious about this distant relative who was completely unknown to her.

Essie considered. 'Samuel's a brusque, quite domineering man. Used to giving orders and having them obeyed. He owns ships at Liverpool and has a flourishing company, so perhaps that accounts for his manner and sense of importance. But, by contrast, Samuel's wife is an absolute delight!

'Amanda's the most charming and kind woman. She cared for you as tenderly as she would her own child after your parents were lost with the Rhiannon.'

Catriona nodded. She'd been a wee girl sailing from America with her parents when the Rhiannon struck a comb of savage rocks just a few, short miles out of home harbour.

Rhiannon was one of Samuel Espley's own ships, heavily laden with cargo bound for Liverpool, and carrying less than a dozen passengers. Only a handful of survivors were rescued from the turbulent sea that raged about the heaving, doomed wreck – Catriona was one of them.

Samuel Espley had claimed Rhiannon was deliberately wrecked by her captain. There'd been investigations and a trial. Captain Chappel was found guilty of his crime and imprisoned for a life sentence. Catriona had been told all these things by Essie McPherson, but she recalled none of it.

'Tell me about Pelham, Granny,' Catriona said, hugging her knees. 'What is the house like?'

'I visited only once, but I remember Pelham as a simply beautiful place!' Essie recalled. 'Very grand and fashionable. Filled with music and elegant furniture and fine paintings – your Aunt Amanda has exquisite taste. And she's very accomplished. Amanda sketches and plays and sings.'

Catriona's hazel eyes were shining with excitement. 'When shall I set off?'

'Oh, as soon as can be arranged, I think.'

Catriona rose from her cushion and crossed to the bureau by the window. As she rolled up the lid, she glanced out across the village to the Pierce house.

And the wonder of those fleeting moments at the loch when Gilbert had tried to kiss her flooded back...

## CHAPTER THREE

It was a fine morning and spring sunshine was melting the last of the lochside snows and dancing across scattered drifts of wild flowers in Essie McPherson's wee cottage garden, when Catriona neatly placed the last of her belongings into the sturdy bag she was taking to Friars Quay.

Her trunk had already been stowed on to the box of the coach which would carry Catriona from Strathlachie and south as far as the Borders. She then had to change coach for the remainder of her journey.

'Nearly ready, pet?' Essie McPherson asked cheerfully, coming into Catriona's room. 'My, you do look bonnie! And suddenly all grown up, going away on your first trip and–' She broke off in consternation, as her granddaughter ran into her arms, just like she

20

had so often as a wee girl.

'Why, Catriona – whatever's this long sad face in aid of?'

'Oh, I shall miss you, Granny!' Catriona exclaimed, hugging her grandmother tightly. 'And Gilbert, and Sophy!'

'Of course you will, and we'll miss you, pet,' Essie said sensibly as they started through into the parlour.

She went to the bureau by the window, taking out a small, oval brooch. The amethysts glowed softly in the sunlight, warm and precious in their setting of rich, old gold.

'This is for you, pet.'

'But, Granny!' Catriona breathed in astonishment. 'It's Mother's brooch – the one Papa gave her when they became betrothed!'

Essie gently pressed the amethyst brooch into Catriona's hands. 'Be sure to wear it in happiness, pet. Ah, here's Sophy come to say goodbye!'

Catriona followed her grandmother's gaze through the window and saw Sophy Hamilton hurrying up the path.

'I did think we'd be seeing Gilbert this morning,' Essie ventured tactfully. 'Is he not coming to see you off?'

'We've said our goodbyes, Granny,' Catriona replied, hesitating slightly before adding, 'When I come back from Friars Quay, Gilbert wants us to be married.'

'And what do you want?' Essie asked softly.

Catriona met her grandmother's eyes steadily. 'I love him, Granny.'

'That's all that matters,' Essie smiled.

'Thank you, Granny!' Catriona gave her grandmother a final hug before answering Sophy's impatient knock at the cottage door.

'Take care!' Essie McPherson called later from the step as she watched Catriona climb up into the coach.

'Come home to me soon, pet.'

Catriona was making the long journey un-chaperoned, and as the days slipped by and the miles rattled away beneath the coach team's hoofs, she soon became seasoned to travelling alone and fending for herself.

'Friars Quay!' the driver called, eventually turning the blowing horses into an inn yard.

Catriona alighted from the coach stiffly, stamping the cramp from her feet. There was no sign of her aunt or uncle, or of a carriage to meet her.

'I'll put your goods over here, shall I, miss?' The driver smiled at her kindly, setting Catriona's luggage down next to a bench beside the coaching-inn's side door, then shouted, 'Good-day to you, miss!'

Catriona returned the driver's cheery farewell, watching the coach with its few remaining passengers trundle onwards to Liverpool as she settled down on the bench to wait for the Espleys' carriage.

A distant church clock struck the hour, and Catriona shifted uneasily. Where on earth was the carriage from Pelham?

The afternoon was already closing, and although the actual coastline was not within sight, Catriona could certainly feel the cold mist rolling in off the sea. Its dampness was seeping through the layers of her clothing, chilling her to the marrow. She shivered, envying the blacksmith the heat of the blistering fire that flared within the open-sided forge across the inn yard.

The glowing coals threw florid light up onto the smith's sweat-streaked face and burly arms as he pounded a white-hot, iron shoe into shape on the sparking anvil. The smith occasionally half-turned to exchange comments with a tall, dark man whose face Catriona could not distinguish, for he stood away from the spitting fire in the gloom of the forge.

Whatever reason was causing the Espley's carriage to be so delayed, Catriona was unwilling to wait any longer in the gathering dusk. The few coins in her purse were all that was left of the small sum Essie McPherson had been able to spare her for travelling expenses, and this certainly wouldn't be sufficient to hire a carriage and driver – even if these were available at such a poor establishment as Friars Quay Inn.

That left only one alternative.

Taking hold of her bulky bag, Catriona strode purposefully along the yard past the forge to the livery stable, where the boy with a mongrel collie was forking fresh straw into the middle stall.

'Excuse me,' Catriona began clearly. 'Can you direct me to Pelham, please?'

'Reckon I know where it is, if that's what you mean, miss,' he replied with a cheeky grin, nodding in the direction of a broad, dusty track winding away from the inn. 'Go down that road there, and keep going till you get to the shore. Then you'll see Pelham. Great big house it is. You can't miss it.

'But it's a fair few miles away,' the lad finished. 'You'll not make it a'fore dark, not if you're walking.'

'I don't have much choice!' Catriona smiled wryly. 'Would you kindly ask the innkeeper if I may leave my trunk here, until someone from Pelham can fetch it for me?'

'No need to ask him, miss,' the lad answered. 'Jack Lippitt won't mind. I'll see to it for you. My name's Huddy Unsworth, miss.'

'Well, thank you for your help, Huddy.'

Catriona considered the stable boy a moment. He could be no older than eight or nine. Impulsively, Catriona reached into her purse and took out two of the coins, pressing them into Huddy Unsworth's cold, grimy hand.

'Thanks, miss!' His face lit up, scarcely able to believe his unexpected wealth as he turned the coins over and over between his fingers.

Catriona started onto the beach road, but Huddy called her back.

'Miss! Hey, miss!' he caught her up, the excited dog capering around his ankles. 'See that bloke in the smithy there?

'He's Morgan – hired hand out at Pelham. Wait here while I tell him.' Huddy sprinted back towards the forge. 'Happen he'll drive you down there.'

Even in the dull nether light betwixt day and night, Catriona could not mistake the frown upon the broad-shouldered man's face as he strode unhurriedly across the yard towards her.

'I'm Morgan, miss. The Espleys' hired man.' He raised his faded, broad-brimmed hat politely, and Catriona saw that his strong hands were lean and calloused from hard, unremitting labour. The skin of his hands and face was dark, tanned by sea and wind and the harsh weathers of this cragged coast, and yet Morgan clearly was not local-born, for Catriona recognised distinct traces of a soft Welsh lilt in his low voice.

'The lad tells me you're bound for Pelham, miss?'

'Yes. I arrived with the afternoon coach. The Espleys are expecting me, and I believed their carriage would meet me,' Catriona explained briefly. 'As you can see, it has not. I was about to begin walking to Pelham, however Huddy warns me the house is some distance away.'

'That it is, miss,' Morgan commented evenly. There was an uncanny, almost luminous blueness to his eyes that Catriona had noticed immediately. His steady gaze was not for a moment leaving her face, and while Morgan's tone gave away nothing of his thoughts, Catriona could see from his eyes that he disbelieved her story.

'So the Espleys are expecting you, miss?'

'They are,' Catriona returned irritably.

She was cold and exhausted and in no mood to have her word doubted. 'Can you drive me out to Pelham or not?'

'I could do that,' he said, without making any movement. 'However, the master is away from Pelham at present, and Mr Julian is out and likely won't be back this side of morning. There's nobody out at the house, miss.'

'This doesn't make any sense!' Catriona exclaimed in exasperation. 'I tell you, I'm expected for a visit. The Espleys are my late father's cousins. I'm Catriona Dunbar–'

'Dunbar?' Morgan echoed sharply, his blue eyes glinting in the half-light and drilling into her.

'You recognise the name?' Catriona queried, flinching uncomfortably beneath his penetrating stare.

Morgan shrugged. 'I heard it once, miss,' he replied carelessly. 'A long time ago.'

Turning away from her, he started with easy, measured strides across the murky yard. 'Soon as the horse is ready, we'll get on our way, miss.'

Morgan duly harnessed the horse between the shafts of the heavy wagon and loaded Catriona's trunk into the wagon-bed.

'My apologies for not bringing the carriage, miss,' he remarked, helping Catriona up on to the rough, wooden seat. 'I wasn't given orders to meet the coach.'

'I just don't understand it!' Catriona reflected, as Morgan climbed up into the seat beside her. 'It was at Uncle Samuel's own invitation that I am here at all!'

'Happen the master confused the date you were arriving, miss,' Morgan commented, lacing the worn reins through his long fingers. 'Since the accident, the Master's not always … well.'

'Accident?' Catriona echoed. 'What accident?'

'It's years past, miss. I was still a boy, but I remember it happening well enough,' Morgan returned evenly. 'The Master was out diving. The current caught him and swept him onto the rocks. He was badly crushed.'

Catriona shook her head sadly. 'I had no idea.'

'Like I say, miss. It's years past. The Master's able to get about well enough now.'

'You said there was no-one at Pelham,' Catriona began after a few moments had elapsed. She was feeling more and more perplexed by the whole situation.

'But what of Mrs Espley, my Aunt Amanda, and Cousin Lucy? Are they away from home, too?'

'Like I said, miss,' Morgan answered quietly. 'There's nobody at Pelham tonight.'

The wagon lurched, bouncing over a hummocky rise, and suddenly the ocean lay before Catriona. Its curling, white-ragged waves rising and rolling up the deserted shore, thumping softer than a sigh against algaed rocks that gleamed silvery in the cold moonshine.

Catriona caught her breath, awed by the spectacular beauty of rippling sea and night sky.

'First time at the coast, miss?' Morgan asked, seeing her response.

'The first I recall,' Catriona answered, inhaling deeply the tangy, salt air. 'I was at Pelham for a while when I was a wee girl, but I don't remember anything about that visit. Not even all of this!' she enthused excitedly. 'Oh, Morgan – it's magnificent!'

'Aye, she's beguiling and gentle as a lover tonight,' Morgan admitted, his even white teeth flashing in an amiable grin. 'But you just wait until she's wild and angry and jealous – no matter how hard you try, you won't shut out from your ears the roar of the tide nor the howling north-westerlies that drive her.'

'I'm sure I shall adore the sea whatever her

mood!' Catriona laughed.

Morgan raised a dark eyebrow. 'The sea's like a fever, miss,' he went on, and although his tone was still carefree, Catriona saw the humour fading from Morgan's eyes. 'Once she's in your blood, you're bewitched and never free of her again.'

'That's a strange thing to say–' Catriona began in surprise, but even as she spoke, they reached a fork in the sandy track, and Morgan turned the wagon away from the beach into a dark avenue of still-naked sycamore and elm which loomed black and skeletal against the sky.

'Must we go in just yet?' she asked. 'I'd like to watch the sea a little longer.'

'Low tide tonight, miss.' Morgan spoke almost as though thinking aloud. 'Nothing happens on a quiet night like this…' Morgan jumped down from the wagon to open the tall, ornately-wrought iron gates into Pelham.

The house reared up before her from dense shadow.

Catriona had never seen a more sombre, less welcoming sight.

'This is Pelham.' Morgan's voice was un-characteristically harsh. 'Home and haunt of the Espleys–'

Morgan drove the wagon through an archway and around to the rear of the house. Instantly, they were bathed in the almost supernatural light of moon and sea, and Catriona saw that the gardens sloped straight downwards to the shore fields. Morgan drew the wagon close to a huge laurel hedge sprawling unchecked against the stone blocks of the wall, almost covering the narrow mullioned windows of wash-house and kitchen.

'I don't know what I'm to do with you, miss,' Morgan said, opening the low kitchen door and respectfully bidding Catriona enter.

'The maidservant Eliza will be long gone home to the village. And what with Mr Julian and the master both being out, Hannah – she's the housekeeper – took the chance to slip away and visit her brother over at Sandford.'

Morgan lit the thick stump of candle standing on the mantel, and bent to throw more kindling onto the dying fire, raking it until the dry logs caught and flared.

'So there's nobody to attend to you, miss. Nobody here at all but thee and me.'

'That's all right, Morgan. I can take care of myself,' Catriona replied, drawn close to the hearth by the warmth of the fire. She stood next to Morgan, stretching out her cold hands gratefully to the heat from the glowing logs.

'Happen there's soup or suchlike on the stove or somewhere,' Morgan began, glancing around the kitchen awkwardly. 'Hannah usually leaves something for whenever Mr Julian gets back.'

Catriona frowned into the crackling blaze. There was nothing else to do but try to make the best of her dilemma. She had warmth and shelter, and would find the makings of a simple supper. If need be, she could sleep on the oak settle here in the kitchen.

Morgan brought in her trunk from the wagon, setting it down onto the stone-flagged floor.

'Will there be anything else, miss?'

'Er, no. Thank you, Morgan,' Catriona replied, hesitating as to whether it would be proper to invite him to share some hot tea with her.

'I shall get off then, miss,' he said, taking his hat from where he'd left it on the wood box. 'If you should need anything, my room's just yonder. Over the stables, see...'

Morgan broke off, as light footsteps tripped quickly down the back stairs towards the kitchen.

Catriona glanced at him quickly. 'You said there wasn't anyone else here?'

'Happen there shouldn't be, miss,' Morgan remarked drily, but Catriona observed he wasn't in the least surprised when a mousy-haired girl of about sixteen burst excitedly into the kitchen – stopping abruptly in her tracks, the eager smile instantly disappearing from her elfin face when she confronted Catriona and Morgan standing there.

'I reckon we're not who you were expecting to see, eh, Eliza?' Morgan half-grinned at the maidservant. 'Well, since you're still here, happen you'll take care of Miss Catriona. She's the master's guest.'

'The master's guest?' Eliza repeated. 'I wasn't told to expect any guest, and besides, I should've gone home hours ago.'

'Then why are you still here?' Morgan enquired bitterly. 'As if I needed to ask!'

Morgan unlatched the door and cold, salt air rushed into the kitchen.

'Good-night, miss,' he said, pausing on the threshold to cast a scathing glance at the sullen maidservant. 'You'd best show Miss Catriona to her room, Eliza.'

Eliza's attention returned to Catriona, her pale eyes narrowing suspiciously.

'Was Morgan telling me right? Are you really the master's guest?'

Catriona didn't begin to comprehend the

emphasis Eliza placed upon the question, but she nodded wearily.

'My father and Mr Samuel Espley were cousins.'

'So you're kin then?' Eliza exclaimed, the tension leaving her curt voice. 'Sort of cousin yourself, like? To the master's son, and daughter, that is?'

'I suppose.'

'Right then.' Eliza began to bustle efficiently about the kitchen, laying plates and cutlery upon the bare table and fetching a tray of cold pie, bread, cheese and slicing onions from the pantry.

'Hannah – she's the housekeeper, miss – didn't say you were coming, so I've no room ready for you. Anyhow, you get on and eat your supper while I light the fire in Miss Lucy's old room and put a few hot bricks into the bed – all ready for when you go up...'

That night, in spite of her weariness, Catriona lay wakeful. The air within the room was stale. The acrid smell of dust and mildew clung to the drapes and linen, and Catriona had the distinct impression that this evidently once-comfortable room had been shuttered and unused, forgotten, almost, for a very long while.

Catriona had placed the precious, amethyst brooch upon the dressing-table where she could see it as she lay huddled in the cold bed.

Long-ago, fond memories of her grandmother, her home, her dear friends, crowded in upon Catriona's over-tired mind. Everything she cared for seemed so hopelessly far away and beyond reach.

Catriona shivered, closing her eyes tightly to shut out the homesickness and the damp chill, finally cocooning the counterpane about her and creeping from the bed to the hearth, where she curled up, willing sleep to come.

But during that long first night at Pelham, thoughts of Gilbert were all that warmed Catriona's cold and lonely heart.

## CHAPTER FOUR

Catriona wakened stiff and chilled the following morning. Cold, grey daylight was seeping into the room, and with a start Catriona realised that despite everything, she'd slept much later than usual.

Lying still for a moment, she could hear the normal household sounds of someone moving about downstairs, doors opening and closing, the clattering of pans and plates.

Catriona rose, washing in the cold water from the pitcher, and dressed quickly in her warmest clothes. Her fingertips lingered fondly upon the amethyst brooch as she pinned it securely at the neck of her sturdy, homespun bodice.

Her room must be almost directly above the kitchen, because down below were the cobbled yard and stables, and the age-greened stone archway through which the wagon had entered.

Morgan was down in the yard, bent over the wood-chopping block as he skilfully hewed a new spoke for one of the wagon's large wheels, which stood propped at his side.

Catriona watched him idly, twisting her hair in thick braids. However, she quickly stepped back from sight as Eliza emerged from the blackthorn patch which wound around from the side of the stables.

A broad grin spread across Eliza's pert face when she spotted Morgan. Leaving the earth path, her footsteps rang quick and light upon the cobbles, and Morgan glanced up at Eliza's approach.

Catriona couldn't hear the words the pair exchanged, but she saw Eliza start to laugh, swinging her full hips so she nudged against Morgan's shoulder as he bent once more to his work. With a final, bantering quip, the maid ruffled Morgan's shock of blue-black hair and sauntered on towards the house.

Catriona guessed they must be sweethearts, and with an earnest wish to be back together with her own sweetheart, she fleetingly appraised her reflection in the glass before going downstairs.

At the foot of the wide, turned staircase, rooms opened off upon either side. Catriona could hear activity, and smell bread baking, and so wandered down a narrow passage way until she came to the kitchen door, beyond which two women were gossiping.

'I don't remember her name exactly – something queer it was,' Eliza was saying, her frown breaking into a wide grin as she paused from turning the heavy handle of the churn.

'Honest, Hannah, when I first come down and saw her standing here with her bag and bundles, I reckoned she must be one of Mister Julian's young ladies come looking for him!'

'Mind your tongue, Eliza!' the house-keeper snapped sharply. 'It's not for the likes of you to tittle-tattle about your betters!'

'I was only saying what I thought!' Eliza retorted obstinately.

'Well, don't,' Hannah cautioned, banging another batch of bread dough onto the table. 'If Master Espley catches you talking that way, there'll be trouble!'

'I'm not frightened of the old man,' Eliza declared airily, pulling a ribbon from her mousy hair and retying it. 'Nor the young one, either!'

'One of these days, you'll learn your lesson the hard way, my girl!' Hannah commented, eyeing the young maid critically. 'There's them and there's us. You'd best remember that and get on with your work. That milk won't churn itself into butter!'

Seconds later, Eliza was approaching the door, and Catriona flustered.

She was embarrassed and vexed by what she'd overheard, but wasn't ready to confront the two women in their kitchen, particularly the dour housekeeper.

Catriona darted away, her seeking hand finding the smooth, brass knob of a room across the hall. Hurriedly letting herself inside, she closed the door soundlessly.

At once, Catriona realised she was not alone.

In the gloom of the heavily-shuttered drawing-room, a thick-set man was slumped in a high-backed chair close to the fire, his breathing noisy as he slept.

'Ah, so you're in here, are you, miss?'

Catriona whirled around as the door opened briskly and Eliza strode in.

'We was wondering when you'd come down,' the maid went on chirpily, stepping over the man's sprawled feet to stoke up the fire. 'Hannah said best to let you sleep as long as you wanted. After your long journey and all. Are you hungry?'

Catriona nodded. 'Yes. Very.'

'No need to whisper, miss.' Eliza grinned, cocking her head to the slumbering man. 'He'll not hear you–'

From somewhere to the front of the old house, a heavy door slammed and loud footfalls echoed along the hall.

'Eliza!' the voice was impatient.

'Coming, sir.' She trotted to the doorway as a tall, strong-jawed man in his middle twenties strode in.

'You wanted me, Mister Julian?'

'You'll have to do. Actually, I wanted our noble hired hand.' Julian Espley's forehead creased into an irritated frown. 'Find him, Eliza,' he went on, stripping off his sand-flecked outdoor clothes and giving them to the maid. 'Tell him Bartie Ashmoore and I are taking on the Loxwoods across country this afternoon. Morgan's to have my horses ready by one.'

'Yes, sir.' Eliza bobbed an awkward curtsey and scuttled from the drawing-room.

Julian threw himself down into one of the chairs, and fixed his attention on to Catriona, as though only now noticing her presence.

'Who are you? Surely Hannah hasn't finally wheedled herself a new scullery maid!' Julian demanded wryly. 'Well don't just stand there, girl, take off my boots!'

'I certainly will not!' she returned indignantly. 'Take them off yourself!'

To her astonishment, Julian threw back his head and laughed at her heartily.

'Your voice gives you away! You must be none other than Cousin Catriona!' he exclaimed. 'I was aware that Father had written to your grandmother, but not that he'd invited you to come so soon. How old are you?'

Catriona bridled slightly. 'Fifteen – almost sixteen.'

'You don't look it,' he observed, appraising her. 'Still, you have pretty eyes. And your hair's a handsome enough colour. Your sort often develop into unexpected beauties and so confound even your harshest critics.'

'Do you sum up everyone you meet as if they were horseflesh?' Catriona retorted crossly.

Julian pulled an amused face, rubbing his chin as though seriously considering. 'Actually, I suppose I do. Well, women, at least!'

He jumped to his feet, snapping his heels together and half-bowing. 'Julian Espley. Your servant, miss! Only son and heir to all you see before and around you, may heaven help me!'

He waved vaguely in the direction of the slumbering man.

'That recumbent fellow in his cups is, of course, your Uncle Samuel, owner of the once-illustrious Espley Shipping Line of Liverpool and Master of Pelham.' Julian was prowling around the room, peering on shelves and under tables before triumphantly raising a decanter from beside the fire dogs.

'Ah, splendid! Father hasn't quite drained the cellar dry.' Julian took the crystal decanter by the neck and winked at Catriona conspiratorially before making for the door. 'Purely for medicinal purposes so I might revitalise my strengths for the rigours

41

of the race this afternoon...'

Catriona stood perplexed after he'd gone, deliberating upon what to do, when Samuel Espley suddenly rallied.

He groaned horribly, opening pallid eyes and fixing Catriona's face with a rheumy, unfocused stare.

His hand reached out and clutched at Catriona's skirt. She pulled away in panic, her feet skidding over a walking cane lying on the floor that she hadn't previously noticed.

And with Samuel Espley's ramblings still loud in her ears, Catriona fled up the stairs and into her room. Slamming the door behind her, and turning the great key to lock it fast.

Grabbing her bag, Catriona's trembling hands fumbled with the bindings as she hastily gathered her few belongings and stuffed them inside.

She couldn't stay in this awful place a moment longer. She'd go home.

A shudder of stark realisation overtook Catriona. How could she return to Strathlachie? Her purse was almost empty.

Essie McPherson had scrimped together all of her meagre savings simply to send Catriona to Friars Quay...

Giving Catriona this trip to Pelham meant

so much to Granny, and Catriona had not the heart to hurt the old lady by telling her that the Espley house and family were no longer as she remembered.

Catriona had no choice but to stay and make the best of things.

Washing her flushed face in the cold water, Catriona tidied her hair before going downstairs again.

Taking a deep breath, she straightened her shoulders and went into the kitchen before courage failed her.

'Good-morning,' Catriona said politely, greatly relieved to find the middle-aged housekeeper alone. 'May I have something to eat, please?'

Hannah threw her a sour glance. 'While you're here, you'll eat in the kitchen with us,' she said, pointedly leaving off her pastry-making to fetch a cup and plate from the dresser. 'Dining-room's not used, except on occasion when the Master's fit.'

'Eliza and me are too busy to fuss with a child,' the housekeeper concluded. 'So you'll not be waited on as you're likely used to.'

'I'm not a child. And I'm not accustomed to being waited upon, Mrs – Hannah,' Catriona stressed. There was a firmness in her soft voice that caught the housekeeper's keen attention.

'I can cook, and I'm used to doing chores. I'll be glad to help–'

An almighty crash from across the hall had Hannah pushing past Catriona and out of the kitchen.

She burst into the drawing-room, with Catriona following.

Catriona's hand flew to her mouth in horror at the sight she observed.

Samuel Espley was sprawled upon the floor, floundering and crying out as though in some fevered delirium.

'Amanda … Amanda!' he moaned over and over, his upturned face staring at Hannah.

But his eyes were blank and expression-less, and Catriona realised her uncle really wasn't aware of herself or Hannah at all.

'There, there, Master.' Hannah's voice was uncharacteristically gentle. 'You've taken a nasty fall, that's all. Open the shutters, miss!' she ordered. 'Let's get some light in!'

Catriona obediently pulled back the heavy curtains and unlatched the panelled wooden shutters.

When daylight flooded the gloomy room, Catriona saw her uncle clearly for the first time. It was obvious to her that Samuel Esp-

44

ley had not shaved or changed his clothes for several days, for he was dishevelled and unkempt. His greying hair disarrayed and caked with mud. His shirt and waistcoat badly soiled and stained with liquor and mud.

To Catriona's horror, her uncle suddenly burst into anguished, racking sobs and tears spilled down his face leaving tracks in the grime on his face.

'Take no notice, miss. It's just the drink,' Hannah said matter-of-factly, cradling Samuel's head. 'His grieving was done long ago.'

'He's gashed his face,' Catriona's throat was tight. She could hardly get the words out. 'I'll get some water to bathe the cut.'

'You did right well in there, miss,' Hannah remarked when she and Catriona were back in the kitchen.

The housekeeper considered Catriona's pinched, white face. 'Best sit yourself down by the fire, lass. You look exhausted. I'll brew a fresh pot of tea.'

Catriona sat in the chimney corner. Now that the incident with Uncle Samuel was over, she couldn't stop shaking and gratefully cupped the mug of hot tea into her cold hands.

'Is he always like that?'

Hannah sighed heavily. 'The Master has bad spells, miss,' she replied, setting a plate of piping hot, buttered crumpets beside Catriona. 'Weeks'll go by and he won't set foot from the house. He just stays in that room and drinks.

'Other times, he'll be sober as a bishop. Gets spruced up and drives off in the carriage, and we'll not see him for days on end. He comes back like you saw him,' she finished, sitting across the hearth from Catriona. 'Drunk, his money all gone on liquor and gambling.'

Catriona sipped the scalding-hot tea slowly, trying to understand. 'My uncle was calling for Amanda, and you said his grieving was over long ago,' she began. 'Is my aunt dead, Hannah?'

'Amanda Espley's alive, miss,' the housekeeper replied simply. 'But she's lost to the Master for good and all.'

'Where is she? And Cousin Lucy, too?'

'Gone. One day she just upped and left. Back to her parents in Grassendale, and took little Miss Lucy with her,' Hannah related gravely. 'It was them going that finally broke him.'

'You're fond of my uncle, aren't you?'

46

Catriona asked tentatively.

'Aye, miss. Reckon I am,' Hannah said. 'I'm a fool to myself, because he treats me as bad as he treats everybody else. But you see, I remember him as he used to be.'

'Before my aunt left?'

'Nay, long before that!' Hannah smiled sadly. 'When I were a slip of a lass no older than you, Samuel Espley was young and handsome and he'd made a fortune from shipping cotton and spices and suchlike. He was a fine figure of a man. Active and powerful. And him and your aunt were like newlyweds, even after the bairns came along–' Hannah's voice dropped to a whisper.

'Master and Julian were out sailing and summat happened. An accident. I'm not sure what exactly. Anyhow, young Julian brought him home. Your uncle's body was all twisted and broken. I'll never forget that night. A man like him would rather be in his grave than crippled the way he is. He lost interest in everything.'

'Poor Uncle!' Catriona was suddenly ashamed of how harshly she'd judged him. 'Was that when Aunt Amanda and Lucy left?'

'Oh, no, miss!' Hannah replied in surprise. 'Your aunt loved him all the more. I never heard so much as a cross word between them. One evening they'd been to a ball over at Larks Grange. Came home in high old spirits. Laughing and talking just like they always did. The Master's valet was getting him into bed, and Amanda went into the drawing-room to put her jewels back in the safe.

'Next morning, she'd gone. And she'd taken Lucy with her,' Hannah concluded with a resigned shake of her head. 'Don't ask me why, miss, because I don't know!'

After their exchange, Catriona spent the remainder of the day exploring the desolate rooms of Pelham.

The rambling mansion was sadly run-down and in dire need of thorough refurbishment. The dining-room still contained some exquisite furniture and the library was a fine one although, it pained Catriona to see so many beautiful books neglected to dust and mildew.

She gathered a posy of wild flowers from the overgrown gardens and took them to her room. Their fresh colours seemed to breathe life and brightness, and Catriona was arranging the late daffodils, primroses and bluebells upon her dressing-table when Hannah popped her head around the door.

'The Master's up and about–' The housekeeper looked harassed. 'Dinner's in an hour, miss. And you're to dress.'

She put on her best Sunday floral and went down. Catriona's doubts about her dress were no greater than her nervousness at what her uncle's present condition might be.

Hesitantly entering the drawing-room, she was dumbfounded by the transformation so few hours had wrought in Samuel Espley!

Dressed immaculately for dinner, this distinguished man gallantly rose to his feet, depending heavily upon the canes as he stepped forward to greet her cordially.

'Catriona. Do join us!' Samuel said, adding apologetically. 'Forgive my not meeting you from the coach last evening– Unfortunately, pressing business detained me in Liverpool.'

'Would that have been the grape or the grain?' Julian enquired with a crooked smile. 'Not even you can subdue me this evening, dear Papa!' He laughed. 'Bartie Ashmoore and I soundly out-rode and out-raced those dullard Loxwood brothers this afternoon!'

'Judge Loxwood and his family are friends and neighbours of ours, Catriona,' Samuel explained genially, but the pulse beating at his temple betrayed his annoyance. 'They live at Larks Grange, several miles inland.

Maud Loxwood is a fine, young woman. Perhaps my son will one day have sufficient good manners to drive you over to meet her.

'Now.' Leaning awkwardly on the canes, Samuel Espley offered Catriona his arm. 'Shall we go in to dinner, my dear Catriona?'

Despite the amiable dinner-table atmosphere that her uncle strove to create, Catriona sensed the undercurrent of hostility between Samuel and his son, and she was relieved when finally she was able to retire and leave the men to their port and cigars.

Hours later, when Pelham was silent, Catriona sat in bed reading a book of poetry she'd brought up from the library. However, her choice had been a mistake, for reading the romantic verse made Catriona miss Gilbert all the more, her longing for him all the keener.

Slipping from her room, she tiptoed down to the drawing-room in search of writing materials. Even writing Gilbert a letter would bring him nearer for a while!

Rolling up the lid of the bureau, Catriona quickly found pen and notepaper amongst the cluttered contents, however, as she searched for ink, a crumpled pile of papers slithered from a pigeon hole onto the floor.

Catriona bent to retrieve then. She didn't

mean to pry, but couldn't help see that these were all overdue accounts from tailor, chandler, grocer. All manner of tradesmen and merchants.

Replacing the papers quickly, Catriona hurried back to her room to write Gilbert's letter, never giving the creditors' notes another thought.

## CHAPTER FIVE

In that house, not a day passed without acrimonious rows erupting between father and son. What disturbed Catriona most, was that Samuel and Julian seemed to relish the quarrels and took perverse satisfaction from taunting each other.

Catriona would have returned home immediately, had this been possible. Only Gilbert's letters were making the long weeks at Pelham bearable. The weather was generally warm and fine now, and each day Catriona gladly escaped from the house to wander for hours along the beach, or sought refuge in Hannah's kitchen.

Early one misty morning, Catriona was

curled up in the chimney corner with her book when Morgan came into the kitchen for breakfast. Catriona knew he'd already been up to the village, and she glanced at him hopefully.

'Mail coach is delayed.' He smiled across at her, answering her silent question. 'Won't be in 'til noon tomorrow.'

'Sit yourself down, lad,' Hannah instructed. 'Eliza! Fetch his breakfast!'

'Morgan's one for book-reading too, miss,' Eliza commented, swishing by where Catriona sat. 'Once upon a time he wanted to be a lawyer or some such. Just fancy that!'

'Just fancy you getting on with your chores for once!' Hannah reprimanded sharply. 'Tea'll be ready.'

Eliza banged a plate of hot muffins on to the table and poured Morgan's tea.

'This is the life!' He grinned. 'Waited on hand and foot!'

'Better make the most of it while you can,' she retorted tartly. 'I don't plan on being a maid all my life, y'know!'

Eliza was always giving Morgan the sharp edge of her tongue, but she giggled and flirted with him too. Catriona imagined they must meet secretly somewhere away from Pelham, for after she finished work, Eliza often primped and preened in front of the glass before slipping out into the dark evening.

'You've dawdled long enough,' Hannah commented without turning from the stove to look at the maid. 'Hall's waiting to be cleaned.'

Eliza pulled a face behind the housekeeper's back and flounced from the kitchen.

Morgan had barely touched a mouthful of his meal when the door was flung open and Julian stood framed by the threshold, his pale eyes angry.

'Morgan. I might have guessed to find you in here gossiping like an old woman!' he said irritably. 'Redbird's waiting to be rubbed down. Damn beast threw a shoe coming down the Spinney. Well, don't just sit there, man! Get to it – I'll want Redbird this evening!'

Catriona kept her eyes fixed upon her book, but she felt her face burning with discomfort.

Morgan instantly rose from the table and went out into the yard. Julian pulled off his gauntlets and strode through the kitchen towards the hall.

'I shall be going to the opera this evening,' he told Hannah, much of the annoyance gone from his voice. 'Make sure Eliza has my clothes ready in good time!'

While Hannah was busy in the pantry, Catriona laid aside her book and quietly pouring a fresh mug of tea, took it and Morgan's breakfast out to the stables.

'Miss?' He looked up questioningly as she pushed open the door.

'You haven't touched your breakfast. I brought it out for you,' she began shyly. 'I'm afraid it's gone cold, but I made fresh tea.'

'That was thoughtful of you, miss. Thanks.'

He was rubbing down the sweating mare, and Catriona noticed flecks of dark blood on Redbird's fetlock.

'Is the horse hurt?' she asked in concern, stroking the bay's neck gently.

'Split hoof. Cuts and scratches,' Morgan answered tersely. 'She shouldn't have been ridden after she cast the shoe.'

'Julian rode her when she was lame?' Catriona exclaimed in disbelief. 'But I thought he was a good horseman!'

'So he is, miss. Likely the best in the whole county.' Morgan's quiet voice had a hard edge. 'But when there's a race or a wager to be won, Mister Julian rides like the devil. He lets nothing stand in his way.'

Catriona sat back on her heels in the clean

straw, watching Morgan as he tended the injured mare. 'Why do they fight all the while?' she ventured at last. 'My uncle, and Julian.'

'Too much of the same kind,' Morgan returned simply.

'The same?'

'Aye, and no amount of fighting can ever change that!'

'I'm sorry for Uncle,' Catriona murmured sombrely. 'But I don't like him a bit. I've tried, and I just can't. It's scary when Uncle flies into one of his rages,' Catriona confided dismally. 'But there's something about Julian that really frightens me!'

Morgan watched her for a moment, sitting in the straw with her small hands folded into her lap, her head bowed.

'We've a new foal. Would you like to feed him?' Morgan asked gently.

'Oh, he's beautiful!' Catriona whispered in delight, when the foal was nuzzling his velvety nose into her hand.

'Morgan,' she went on tentatively, for Catriona was aware that servants generally didn't have reading or writing. 'When Eliza said you enjoyed reading, was she speaking truthfully?'

'I like books well enough,' Morgan replied guardedly. 'I inherit that from my mother.

She'd read aloud to my sister and I, and to Pa, too, when he was ashore.'

'Does your family live here in Friars Quay?'

'I lost my mother and sister to the influenza epidemic,' he answered after a moment. 'If my father had his choice, he'd be dead, too.'

'Whatever do you mean?' Catriona was unable to conceal her shocked response.

'Pa's in jail!' Morgan returned bitterly. 'And there he'll stay until he dies!'

'I'm so sorry, Morgan,' Catriona mumbled awkwardly, reaching out her hand to touch his arm. 'It must be awful for you.'

'Worse for him, miss,' Morgan responded, and Catriona saw clearly the pain behind the anger within his deep eyes.

'My father's an innocent man – serving sentence for another man's crime!'

'I have neither time nor inclination to play nursemaid to a child!'

Julian's irate voice carried through the open windows of the drawing-room out on the hot, still air to the garden where Catriona was clearing weeds from a long-neglected flower bed.

'Your cousin is not a child!' Samuel Espley's voice was slurred. He'd been drinking heavily for almost forty-eight hours. 'If you

56

must go to the opera with Ashmoore and his wife, why not take Catriona and Maud with you?'

'Because I don't choose to!'

'You're a fool, Julian!' Samuel railed. 'Wasting your time hacking about with the Ashmoores! Bartie Ashmoore is a witless idiot!'

'Bartie happens to be my closest friend and a distinguished Member of Parliament!' Julian returned, adding scathingly, 'I find political affairs stimulating. You doubtless won't appreciate that, since you locate your own stimulation in the bottom of a glass!'

'You'd be better employed paying some attentions to Maud Loxwood,' Samuel spat. 'Why don't you marry her and be done with it!'

'And make your life easy?' Julian demanded in sarcastic incredulity. 'You won't turn Pelham or Espley Shipping over to my control, so why should I get you off the hook upon which your colossal incompetence has impaled you?

'Yes. I'll marry Maud Loxwood,' Julian concluded savagely, 'when it suits my purposes, and not a day before!'

'If you're not a sight more careful, you'll lose her!'

Vainly trying to shut out the vicious

argument between father and son, Catriona hurriedly finished her gardening and took the curving path down to the beach.

Slipping off her shoes and stockings, Catriona wandered along the deserted beach farther than she'd ever gone before and presently came within sight of a tumbledown boathouse, tucked into a cove and sheltered by the high shelf of dunes and rocks rising behind and around it.

'Morgan!' Catriona shouted, hailing the hired hand as he strode down through the dunes towards the boathouse.

'I didn't know that you had a boat!' she exclaimed breathlessly, running to meet him.

'It's not mine, miss. It belongs to Pelham,' he replied awkwardly, opening up the boathouse to reveal a small boat. 'But nobody there has sailed in it for years.'

Catriona glanced out at the soft waves, lapping beguilingly nearer.

'Are you going sailing today?'

'Aye, just for a short while,' he replied, dragging the boat down the hard sand. 'That mist will likely roll into shore as fog before the afternoon's out.'

'Take me with you!' Catriona implored, her eyes bright with excitement. 'Please, Morgan! I've never been sailing!'

Morgan considered doubtfully before nodding. 'Very well, miss.'

He pushed the boat into the shallows and lifted Catriona aboard before pushing the small craft into deeper water and climbing aboard himself, taking the oars and rowing with smooth, even strokes.

'It's like being inside a picture!' Catriona exclaimed in delight, viewing the coastline as it receded farther and farther.

'There's Pelham – how different it appears from out here. Surely that's the queer crooked chimney of the coaching inn, just visible between the hills?'

'Aye, it is. See over there, on that hilltop–' He pointed to a grassy rise where a solitary, squat cottage sat back amongst a dense thicket of straggling, evergreen bushes.

'That's Gorse Cottage. I lived there with my family. And south of it, where that high point of land juts out to sea like a finger? That's Beacon Point. If the fog comes down, you'll likely see the beacon torches burning.'

'To keep the ships of the rocks, you mean?' Catriona began with interest, breaking off as realisation dawned on her.

'I hadn't even thought, Morgan. Isn't that dreadful. The ship my parents drowned upon must have gone down somewhere near here!'

'Aye, miss,' Morgan said ruefully. 'She did.'

'You know about the Rhiannon?' Catriona asked in surprise.

'My sister, mother and I were watching her coming in from the window of our cottage,' he said solemnly. 'I left them indoors and ran outside. I was on the beach when the Rhiannon foundered on the Combs. That's a drawn-out string of rocks, miss.'

'You saw the wreck?' Catriona's throat was tight.

'I did, miss,' he answered softly. 'The Rhiannon was a sturdy old ship, but she didn't have a chance once she hit the Combs. Neither did most of the good folk aboard.'

As Morgan rowed farther out, swirls of damp mist gradually absorbed their small boat and although they were now quite near the brig at anchor, Catriona could barely make out the ship's bulk.

'Aye – it's the Candeloro all right,' Morgan murmured.

'I saw her – the Candeloro – from the beach. Is she waiting for the wind and the tide?'

'She's waiting right enough, miss,' Morgan commented grimly. 'But not for wind or tide. If I guess right, by morning she'll be gone. And lighter for the night she spent here!'

'There's another boat. A little one like ours!' Catriona exclaimed, her sharp eyes spotting the dark shape. 'There're two of them. They're coming from the Candeloro!'

'Do you see them?' Morgan muttered an oath. 'They're not waiting for night!' he breathed, thinking aloud. 'They're using the fog...'

He suddenly glanced around at Catriona, as though for a few seconds he had forgotten her very presence.

'Lie down flat, miss!' he ordered sharply. 'Don't make a sound. Even a whisper carries like pistol-crack in fog!'

Catriona caught his urgency, and was alarmed. 'What is...?'

Morgan silenced her, his fingertip resting against her lips. 'We must not be seen, miss!'

Catriona lay still on the rough floor of the boat, her muscles tense, her heart pounding at the unseen, unknown danger.

Candeloro's boats passed by so close that Catriona could smell the acrid tobacco of the sailors' pipe smoke. Seconds stretched endlessly until at last Morgan touched her shoulder.

'It's safe. But stay quiet!' he warned, his mouth pressed close to her ear. 'The Candeloro may put out other boats.

'We'll circle through Spinney around to Pelham,' Morgan remarked, when they reached shore. 'Best not to go back along the beach, lest they spot us.'

'Why must we hide from them?' Catriona exclaimed, speaking for the first time. 'Who are they?'

'Smugglers, miss,' he answered shortly.

'You'd been watching the Candeloro.' Catriona looked up from replacing her stockings and shoes. 'You even went out today to be sure it was her. You knew she was a smuggler, didn't you?'

'Miss,' Morgan began, when Catriona had fallen into step alongside him and they were starting through thickly wooded Spinney. 'Smugglers are a cut-throat band. It'd be safest if you don't let on what you've seen this afternoon. And there's something else.' He paused awkwardly, not meeting Catriona's eyes.

'It's not my place to beg a favour, miss – and I don't like to do it, either.'

'What is it, Morgan?' she murmured encouragingly.

'I'd be obliged if you didn't tell that I use the boat,' he said at last.

'Who would I tell? My uncle? Or Julian?' she demanded. 'How can you think I'd ever give you away to them? You're the only person at Pelham who's been kind to me, Morgan! You're my friend!' Catriona cried passionately. 'I would never betray you to anyone!'

'I'm obliged, miss,' he said humbly, looking down into her earnest eyes. 'And I mean you no disrespect but, I can't be your friend, nor you mine. It wouldn't be proper, and the Espleys wouldn't allow it.'

'Because you're their hired hand?' she retorted in disgust. 'That's nonsense, Morgan!'

'It's the way of the world, miss,' he said mildly, guiding her through a copse and out of Spinney.

'It's still nonsense,' Catriona said stubbornly, as the chimneys of Pelham became visible through the drifting fog. 'And whatever my uncle and cousin would say – you're still my friend!'


'Judge Loxwood is outside with some soldier boys!' Eliza called next morning, sauntering along the hall from Pelham's great front door just as Julian was coming downstairs.

'He's looking for the master.'

'So are half the creditors in Liverpool!' Julian grinned, rubbing a hand carelessly over the coarse beard shadow upon his cheek. 'However, since the old man is out on another of his trips, the good judge and his military pals will have to scour every gin-shop between here and New Brighton to find him!'

'I did tell Judge Loxwood no-one at Pelham knew nothing about the smuggling,' Eliza sniffed imperiously. 'But he insists on seeing somebody.'

Catriona crouched on the landing, watching through the balustrade as Julian pulled open the door and went outside. Darting into one of the unused bedrooms, Catriona peered down at the horsemen assembled in the driveway.

There was a middle-aged man dressed in civilian clothes, whom she assumed to be Judge Loxwood, and the Captain of the Command who led a party of four soldiers.

Julian and the judge were conversing, Julian shrugging and shaking his head.

Judge Loxwood was nodding gravely, and the party turned to leave.

Catriona wandered across to her own room and found Eliza there putting clean linen onto the bed.

'For all his fancy talk about smashing the smugglers and the wreckers,' Eliza commented sagely. 'The judge'll not catch them, y'know. He never has and he never will.'

'Why not?' Catriona queried.

'Because they're clever – and because local folks cover up for 'em!'

'Isn't that dangerous?'

'Well of course it's dangerous, miss!' Eliza retorted scornfully. 'Smugglers or anybody caught helping them hangs for sure. But you see, the smugglers bring goods folk couldn't afford else ways. And don't run away with the idea it's only poor folks mixed up in it, either! There's half the gentry in the county filling their cellars with smuggled liquor. Not Judge Loxwood though,' the maid concluded disparagingly. 'A long streak of misery, he is. Just like that old maid daughter of his!'

'What's Maud like?' Catriona asked curiously.

'Dull as dishwater.' Eliza gave an acid reply. 'And the wrong side of thirty.'

'Julian must love her,' Catriona said.

'Why? Because he's marrying her?' Eliza demanded sarcastically. 'He'll only wed her for the dowry she brings with her.'

'Whoa!' Morgan slowed the horse on the road from Friars Quay village to Pelham, bringing the wagon to a standstill alongside

65

the hedgerow where Catriona was picking berries.

'Blackberry and apple pie for tea, is it, miss?'

'Preserves!' Catriona smilingly returned. 'Hannah said I can put up some jars to take home for Gilbert and Granny. Actually, I've been looking out for you to come,' she added, gazing up at him hopefully. 'Is there–'

'Aye, there is, miss!' He laughed, taking the letter from his pocket and handing it to her.

'At last!' Catriona exclaimed jubilantly, however her face fell as she recognised the handwriting. 'Oh! It's from Sophy!'

'Wasn't there anything else?'

'Not today,' Morgan answered sympathetically. 'You were expecting something from your young man?'

Catriona nodded bleakly. 'I haven't heard from Granny for a while, but Gilbert always writes so regularly – I just can't understand why I haven't had a letter from him for weeks!'

'Must be hard for you,' Morgan commented, steadying the horse as a hare darted across her path and away down into the dunes. 'Being parted from him.'

'It's awful, Morgan! I never imagined I could miss anybody so badly,' Catriona confessed ardently.

'Not long to wait, miss.' Morgan smiled. 'You'll be off home at the end of next month.'

'It seems an eternity away!' she grimaced, taking up the basket brimming with plump blue-black berries. 'May I come back with you?'

'Surely!' He sprang down, and helped Catriona up onto the wagon seat.

'Morgan, you can read and write, you know about the sea and ships and horses and gardening and carpentry and a host of other crafts,' Catriona began when they were jogging out towards the shore. 'Why do you remain at Pelham?'

'My schooling was cut short, miss,' Morgan answered after a moment. 'I stay to complete my education.' He smiled wryly. 'I borrow books from Pelham's library. They're not missed because neither of the Espleys have set foot in that room since your aunt left!'

'You're teasing me,' Catriona reproved. 'That can't be the only reason!'

'It's one of them. I do intend learning more, and Pelham's the place for me to do that,' Morgan said seriously. 'I've nothing of my own, miss. Not a farthing. Finding work elsewhere wouldn't be easy for someone like me.'

'Because of your father, you mean?' Catriona enquired tentatively.

Morgan inclined his head reluctantly. 'There are people who believed in my father's innocence. Your Aunt Amanda did, and Judge Loxwood, too.'

Morgan drove the wagon through Pelham's gates and around the drive into the archway.

'He presided over Pa's trial and could've ordered execution instead of a life sentence–'

Redbird's hoofbeats galloped hard up alongside them, and Julian reined in to a canter as he passed the wagon.

'Had a pleasant afternoon with your playmate, Catriona!' He grinned, dismounting and leaving the mare sweating and blowing as he strode for the house. 'At least while Morgan's entertaining you, he's earning his keep... Lord knows, he's precious little use at anything else!'

Catriona scrambled from the wagon and raced after Julian, her blood boiling. 'How dare you, Julian!' she exploded the instant they were indoors.

Julian calmly ignored her outrage, stripping off his coat and shirt and tossing them across a chair back as he crossed to the sink.

'Be a good girl and fetch me a pitcher of hot water.'

'Heat it yourself. You know where the fire is!' Catriona retorted, incensed by his arrogance. 'And you shouldn't be washing in the kitchen – Hannah doesn't like it.'

'Hannah is a servant – just like Morgan Chappel,' Julian remarked, lifting the copper of warmed water to the sink. 'Morgan has obviously impressed you greatly with his skills. However, they wouldn't take him very far if I had a fancy to dismiss him from Pelham. A jail-bird's son without references would either starve or submit to the workhouse.' He laughed unpleasantly. 'It might be a diverting experiment to discover which fate awaits Morgan.'

'You are despicable, Julian!' Catriona breathed, her angry eyes aflame. 'Morgan's twice the man you are, or ever could be!'

Julian towelled down, his attention rivetted upon the hot brilliance her furious indignation was bringing to Catriona's eye and cheek.

'Well, well. Life is certainly filled with surprise,' he murmured in a slow voice. 'Our country kitten has some sharp claws!'

Even as rage against him burned from deep within her, Catriona was very aware that Julian was looking at her in a way he never had before.

Hannah gave a relieved sigh as she closed the door against the blustery autumnal day.

'Happen we'll get some peace and quiet now Master Julian's off to stay with the Ashmoores,' she commented, returning to her baking board. 'Mind, I'm not sure I wouldn't rather the Master was ranting and raving instead of mouldering round miserable as second skimmings like he is now.'

'He seems to be getting worse,' Catriona said from the chimney corner where she was toasting her toes by the fire.

'Don't reckon he'll ever get better, miss,' Hannah said grimly. 'Doctor's warned him, but he pays no heed.

'Last night when Morgan was getting him upstairs, I swear if the Master could've got to his own feet, he'd have flattened the lad good and proper!'

'How long has Morgan been at Pelham, Hannah?'

'Just after Morgan's father was arrested, Mrs Chappel and her daughter took influenza and died,' Hannah explained. 'Morgan was only a lad and he got sent to the orphanage.

'Your Aunt Amanda took pity on him and rescued him. Brought him to Pelham. Made him just like one of the family.' Hannah's mouth tightened into a straight line. 'Even had him taught lessons alongside Mister Julian.'

'Is that why Julian hates Morgan so?' Catriona asked quietly. 'Because he was jealous?'

'What young gentleman wouldn't be, miss?' Hannah demanded stiffly. 'A lad like Morgan – whose father done what Arfon Chappel done – brought in and treated like royalty! Wasn't proper, miss. Anyhow, when Amanda left Pelham – things were soon set to rights.'

'You mean that Morgan was banished to the stables,' Catriona added coldly. 'And forced to become the Espleys' hired hand!'

Hannah sniffed. 'Morgan's a good enough lad, I'll not say different, but when all's–'

She was interrupted by a hasty rapping at the kitchen door.

'I'll answer it.' Catriona went to the door. 'Why, hello, Huddy!'

'How do, miss.' The wee lad from the coaching inn was breathing hard from running. 'Letter for you, miss. I got told to bring it to you quick.'

Catriona was transfixed by the sombre black edging to the letter. Her heart froze. Snatching the letter from Huddy's grimy hands, she frantically tore it open.

'Miss. You've gone white as a sheet!' Hannah bustled to her side.

'Granny.' Catriona was trembling, her legs suddenly unable to support her. 'She's … she's…'

'Sit yourself down.' Hannah pushed Catriona into a chair.

'No! No, I can't,' Catriona protested agitatedly, struggling unsteadily to her feet. 'I must go home straight away, Hannah.'

'Nay, nay, miss – calm down!' Hannah returned sensibly. 'We don't even know when the next coach is due!'

'I don't care. I have to get home!' Catriona cried desperately.

''Course you do, miss,' Hannah agreed quickly. 'You sit down before you fall down. I'll go up and pack your bits.

'Soon as Morgan's back from driving Mister Julian's luggage to the Ashmoores, he can take you to the coach.'

'You're not going anywhere, Catriona!'

Both women turned as though struck. Neither one had noticed Samuel Espley listening from the doorway into the hall.

'Uncle. It's Granny,' Catriona explained brokenly, starting past him to the hall. 'I'm going home.'

'I told you–' Espley grasped her wrist tightly, forcing her back around to face him. 'You are not leaving this house!'

Catriona stared at him with sorrowful eyes. 'You don't understand, Uncle,' she began patiently. 'I'm taking the next coach north.'

'Your grandmother is dead.' Espley's voice was hard, void of emotion. 'I'm your legal guardian now. And you will stay at Pelham!'

'I won't ... I won't...' Cartiona shook her head over and over again, backing away from Samuel Espley, tears of pain spilling uncontrollably from her eyes. 'I'm not a prisoner. You can't keep me here!'

Spinning around, she tore open the kitchen door and fled across the garden.

Catriona ran and ran until her heart was hammering and her lungs felt they must surely burst. Stumbling to her knees, she crumpled to the coarse grass of the dunes and gave vent to her grief and helplessness...

It was there that Morgan found her as night darkened the shore.

'I've just got back from the Ashmoores. Hannah told me,' he muttered, kneeling at Catriona's side as she lay face down, her head buried into her folded arms. 'I'm so very sorry, miss.'

Morgan reached out his hand, gently touching her shoulder. 'Dear Lord, you're half-frozen–'

Pulling off his coarse-woven coat, Morgan lifted Catriona's frail, trembling body, and gently wrapped the thick garment about her.

'I wish there was something I could say to make the hurt less,' he whispered, chafing her icy hands within his own. 'But there isn't, Catriona. There isn't a single thing.'

'Oh, Morgan!' Catriona raised dry, anguished eyes to him. 'She was all alone. I wasn't there!'

Morgan impulsively pulled Catriona's shivering body hard against his chest, wrapping his arms tightly about her as much to warm as to comfort her.

## CHAPTER SIX

'Don't torment yourself, miss,' Morgan advised some weeks later. 'It wasn't your fault you weren't allowed to attend your grandmother's burial,' he went on, splitting another log into kindling. 'She'd understand.'

'I know,' Catriona responded unhappily.

'It just hurts so much that I wasn't there when she needed me.'

She was desperate to go home to Scotland, but Samuel Espley remained utterly relentless.

'I haven't heard from Gilbert since his letter of condolence,' she told Morgan later as they shared a luncheon of bread and cheese from his snap tin. 'But will you mail this for me? I've written to Gilbert, asking him to come and fetch me home.

'Gilbert is to be my husband – Uncle Samuel must listen to him, mustn't he?' Catriona asked forlornly. 'Gilbert is my last hope!'

While Catriona counted the days, willing Gilbert's response to come speedily, she drew strength from knowing that soon she would leave Pelham for ever and become Gilbert's wife. Only the notion of also leaving behind her dear friendship with Morgan Chappel caused Catriona regret.

For the first time in months, smugglers had been on Friars Quay beach the previous night. From her window, Catriona had spied them masked and silent, moving from the water's edge and away amongst the cover of the dunes with their kegs of contraband.

Catriona was sitting at her window now, repairing the seam of her thick, plaid skirt.

She saw Julian galloping into the yard on Redbird, returning from his stay with the Ashmoores.

'May I come in?' he asked, a quarter hour or so later, sauntering through the open doorway. 'I've just got back.'

'I saw you,' Catriona remarked indifferently. 'Did you enjoy your visit?'

'It was first rate. Stayed weeks longer than I planned.' He grinned enthusiastically. 'Ended up in London, and had a good time of it, too!'

Julian paused, clearing his throat almost apologetically. 'The old man's just told me about your grandmother. It's rotten luck.'

'Yes,' Catriona replied shortly.

'If it's any consolation, I think the old man was wrong to keep you from attending the funeral,' Julian offered seriously. 'Whether he admits it or not, my father is no longer master of Pelham. If I had been here, I would've put you aboard the coach to Scotland myself!'

'Would you really?' Catriona queried, her eyes flashing challengingly. 'Then do so now, Julian!' she cried. 'Defy your father. Take me to the coaching inn!'

Julian hesitated, his face dark with annoyance.

'Your silence answers me, Julian!' Catriona railed in disgust. 'I was once told you and your father are two of the same kind. And it's true!'

Julian leaned back against the mantel and surveyed Catriona with a sardonic grin. 'Anything else, sweet cousin?'

'You're weak, Julian! You're a selfish, mean-spirited bully! And worse, you're a liar and a cheat. You're deceiving Maud Loxwood!'

'Careful, Catriona!' Julian warned in a low voice. 'You're going too far, girl.'

But Catriona would not be stopped. 'I've never met Maud, but she deserves better than to be betrayed! Morgan says she's a fine girl and–'

'Morgan says?' Julian echoed vehemently, all humour gone. His young cousin's stinging taunts had found their mark, and Julian's anger was cold and dangerous. 'You regard Morgan Chappel as such a shining, honourable knight, don't you? So I'm certain he's told you all about his past.'

'He has. And that his father's in prison is no fault or shame of Morgan's!' Catriona cried loyally.

'I do admire your charity,' Julian continued slyly. 'I'm sure I couldn't be so magnanimous if my parents had drowned in

77

the ship Morgan's father scuppered!'

Catriona ill-concealed her shock at Julian Espley's revelation.

The instant Julian left her room, Catriona sped down to the stables and waited in mounting agitation for Morgan to arrive back from Friars Quay village.

'Why didn't you tell me?' She waylaid him at the doors. 'I trusted you. I believed you were my friend!' Catriona shook her head despairingly. 'I opened my heart to you and you deceived me!'

Morgan searched Catriona's troubled face in consternation.

'Catriona. It isn't as it appears,' he said at last. 'I didn't ever lie to you.'

'Nor did you tell me the truth!' she cut in quietly. 'We've spoken about my parents – the way they died. Why didn't you tell me your father was Rhiannon's captain?'

'In the beginning, I thought you must know,' Morgan answered simply. 'Then, well, how could I just come out and say something like that? And later, when we really became friends–' His eyes fleetingly met hers. 'I had started to hope that it wouldn't matter so much to you, Catriona.'

'Wouldn't matter!' she cried, her voice rising shrilly. 'Your father killed my parents!'

Morgan's response could not have been more acute had she struck him. 'My father's innocent, miss,' he said curtly, fighting to restrain his own emotions. 'However, suppose he were guilty, would that make me guilty, too?

'For all your noble talk of loyalty and friendship, you're no better than the rest!' Morgan said bitterly, his taut resolve ultimately breaking. 'You're looking at me now, Catriona, but all you can see is the hired hand who's a jail-bird's son!'

He strode away from her, as an afterthought turning and taking a letter from his coat.

'Sorry, miss. I was almost forgetting. There's a letter for you.'

Morgan's attitude was deliberately servile, but his eyes were blazing with contempt, and Catriona was unable to meet their searing gaze as she stepped forward to receive the long-awaited reply from Gilbert.

Catriona stalked stiff-backed from the stables, making for the snow-dusted beach where she could be certain of privacy to read her letter.

Sheltering from the biting north-westerly wind, Catriona sat upon the steps of the boathouse and eagerly began reading

Gilbert's letter.

As she took in the words, Catriona's blood turned to ice in her veins.

*I have to ask you to release me from my promise,* Gilbert wrote formally. *Sophy and I are in love.*

Gilbert and the girl who was dearer than a sister to Catriona?

It wasn't true! It couldn't be. Catriona loved them both so much. They wouldn't hurt her like this.

The words on the page blurred in front of her, but Catriona couldn't weep. She felt numb. As though she'd never be capable of feeling love ever again.

She'd believed herself betrayed by Morgan Chappel. But now, Catriona knew the bitterest betrayal of all.

She remained at the boathouse until the incoming tide brought dark waves crusted with ice up on to the beach and cast them at her feet.

All of Catriona's hopes, her whole life, was tumbling down about her. Even Morgan Chappel's companionship was now lost to her. Catriona knew she must somehow get away.

By midnight, Julian was out and Eliza had gone home. Hannah had retired for the night, and by good fortune, Uncle Samuel was still in the drawing-room slumbering off the effects of his latest jaunt.

Catriona packed a change of clothes and a few personal belongings into a small bundle. The rest of her possessions must be left behind.

In her stockinged feet, Catriona crept down the back stairs, through the kitchen, and with pounding heart, darted out into the cloud-ridden, moonless night and across the cobbled yard to the stables.

Catriona let herself noiselessly into the stables, aware that Morgan was sleeping just a few yards away up in the hayloft. The slightest sound might awaken him and bring him down to investigate. Catriona was so tense she could scarcely breathe, but her determination was steeled.

Resting her bundle into the straw, Catriona padded along the line of stalls, shushing the horses as they stirred and whickered curiously.

'Easy, girl. Easy,' she crooned into the ear of the grey mare, slipping a bridle on to the animal. 'Shhh, it's all right–'

'Catriona!'

A cry of alarm escaped her lips as she felt a hand upon her arm, spinning around to see

Morgan, barefoot and wearing only breeches, his blue-black hair tousled from sleep.

'What are you doing?'

'Leaving Pelham,' she returned, every inch of her as taut as a coiled spring. 'Gilbert's marrying Sophy. But I'm going home to Strathlachie anyway.'

'It's madness, Catriona.' He caught her by the shoulders, bringing her around to face him. 'You can't!'

'Then I'll die trying!' she whispered vehemently. 'You won't stop me, Morgan!'

He held onto her fiercely, staring down into her eyes for a long moment. 'I'll go with you,' Morgan said finally. 'I don't–'

The stables' door flung back on its hinges and a flurry of fine rain blew within. Lantern-light flooded over Catriona and Morgan, and Morgan instinctively drew the girl closer to him as Samuel Espley stood framed by the doorway.

Espley's raddled face contorted with rage as he beheld his niece in the naked arms of the hired hand.

'Saw you sneaking out here,' he mumbled, his words sliding drunkenly one into the next.

'Harlot!' Espley staggered forwards, violently setting aside the lantern so it threw grotesque images leaping and crouching about the stables' stone walls. The horse whip in his hands flicked as Espley reached out for Catriona.

Morgan threw Catriona to the straw as the whip sliced through the air, taking its stinging lash broad across his chest.

'I asked her to meet me, Master!' he shouted, using his body to block Samuel Espley's getting any closer to Catriona.

'Miss wanted to go back to the house. I wouldn't let her go.'

Catriona heard her own voice crying unintelligibly. It was her fault. Not Morgan's! None of it was his fault! Why didn't her uncle hear her, why didn't he stop?

Catriona was down on the ground, her knees drawn tight to her body, staring with horrified eyes as again and again her uncle raised the whip and again and again Morgan Chappel accepted the beating.

Morgan was strong. Why did he not defend himself?

Catriona was helpless to do anything but watch in mute terror as Samuel Espley exorcised the frenzied violence of his drunken wrath.

Breathing thickly, Espley's head dropped onto his chest, his shoulders sagged. Turning, he made awkwardly across the stable, leaning heavily on to his cane. Staring blankly, he half-stumbled out into the drizzle and across the yard to the house.

Catriona leaped to Morgan's side. His back and shoulders were laced with cruel thin cuts and blistered with red weals. He lay sprawled in the straw, horribly still.

'He's not dead, miss.' Eliza sauntered through the open, swinging doors. 'Just passed out.'

Catriona spun around, too relieved at the matter-of-fact reassurance to wonder why the maid was at Pelham so early.

'Help me, Eliza,' she said.

Morgan groaned, shifting slightly. His eyes still closed.

Catriona's every attention snapped back to him, but Eliza was already bustling by her.

'I'll tend to him, miss,' the maid said briskly. 'You go back up to the house.'

'No!' Catriona's refusal was adamant. 'Morgan was beaten because of me.'

'I'm sure he was, miss,' Eliza remarked drily. 'But you can't do no good for him now. The Master'll likely already be sleeping it off and won't remember a thing when he wakes up – but if he should happen to take it into his head to wander out again and he

84

catches you in here…'

The maid sucked in her breath meaning-fully. 'There'd be no stopping him, miss.'

Morgan was starting to come round, and Eliza bent to him, so he was able to lean against her.

'Get yourself into the house, miss.' The maid didn't spare Catriona another glance. 'And stay there!'

Catriona was loath to abandon Morgan. However, there was sense in Eliza's warning about Uncle Samuel. Sick with guilt and remorse, Catriona reluctantly acquiesced.

Pausing at the stable doorway, she watched as, with Morgan's arm draped over her shoulders, Eliza wrapped her own arms about him and helped him to his feet. Catriona was ashamed of the jealousy she felt.

If Samuel Espley did retain any collection of his actions that damp, drizzly night, he made no reference to it.

Sober and groomed, he emerged from Pelham the following morning and bid Catriona a gracious goodbye, was tolerably civil to Morgan as he mounted his horse, and with an amiable nod at Julian, cantered through the archway and away.

'That's the last we'll see of the old man until he's full and his pockets are empty,'

Julian remarked, pausing alongside Catriona on the stone steps.

'I returned too late for last night's excitements,' he went on wryly. 'However, I gather Morgan Chappel took quite a thrashing for your sake! Hmm, you might just be worth it at that, cousin!'

Laughing loudly, Julian disappeared indoors and Catriona went hesitantly to the vegetable garden. Morgan was working as any other day, and the uncharacteristic tension of his muscles and movement were the only indications of the horrible beating he'd suffered for Catriona's sake.

'Are you all right?' she asked him.

'I am,' he replied politely. 'Thank you, miss.'

'Why did you let Uncle Samuel go on believing that you and I were...' Catriona faltered uncomfortably. 'I would've owned up to the truth. Why did you stop me?'

'I know Samuel Espley better than you do, miss. I know what he's capable of,' Morgan replied evenly, never pausing in his work as he spoke.

'The mood Master was in, if he'd learned you were running away, there's no guessing what he would've done! The Master doesn't remember last night, and you and I are the

86

only others who know what happened,' Morgan said firmly. 'It's gone and done with, miss. No cause to say more about it.'

Catriona felt he was dismissing her, but she lingered uncertainly. 'Morgan. Can we go back to the way we were before we quarrelled? Be friends again?'

'That's for you to decide, miss,' he answered unemotionally.

'Perhaps we can't put things back exactly,' she unwillingly conceded. 'But we can begin again, can't we? I don't want to lose your friendship, Morgan!'

He stopped working, and really looked at her. Catriona felt his level gaze upon her, aware that colour was rising to her cheeks as Morgan's clear, blue eyes penetrated to her very soul.

'Nor I yours, Catriona,' he answered at length.

She smiled thankfully up at him, experiencing a kind of shyness she'd never before known with Morgan.

With the coming of spring, Catriona began reviving Amanda Espley's walled flower garden, and spent many contented hours planting and nurturing lavender, primroses and bell flowers.

Grandmother McPherson's cottage had been duly cleared and occupied by new tenants. The village choirmaster, Oliver Stuart, had forwarded a few of Essie McPherson's personal effects to Catriona at Pelham.

Opening the package, and seeing again the few possessions Granny had especially cherished, evoked poignant memories for Catriona. She stood the posy bowl on her mantel, hung the watercolour miniature her mother had painted of Strathlachie's glen upon the wall of her room, began setting the small collection of well-read books on to the shelf.

Catriona thoughtfully considered the volume of Burns, and hurried down to the stables.

'It's beautiful, Catriona!' Morgan responded when she presented him with the book. 'However, I can't possibly accept it!'

'Please do, Morgan,' she insisted quietly.

'But it belonged to your grandmother. It means so much to you!'

'I really want you to have it,' Catriona said, adding with a mischievous smile, 'If it will make you feel easier about accepting, in return for the book, you must promise to read to me the very next time we're out in the boat!'

'Done!' Morgan laughed. 'Although you do realise, I don't have your Scottish accent to do Burns justice!'

'You recite splendidly!' Catriona returned, who thoroughly enjoyed the all too rare occasions when they went sailing and would read poetry, or simply talk.

Still smiling as she left the stable, Catriona nearly collided with Julian as he rode into the yard.

'Ah! Do I detect a certain becoming sparkle in your eye, a revealing lightness to your step, Catriona!' he chided wryly. 'Your cheek tellingly warm with regard for our humble hired hand!'

Julian swung down from the saddle, sidling alongside her.

'Tell me just one thing,' he murmured confidentially. 'Do you like Morgan's hayloft?'

Catriona had never seen, nor set foot in, Morgan's room, although she didn't add to her cousin's amusement by protesting as much. Julian's merciless teasing about her friendship with Morgan no longer stung or embarrassed Catriona as it once had. But she could not truthfully deny the tender feelings the softness of Morgan's voice, the fleeting touch of his hand, the nearness of him whenever they were alone together, provoked within her.

Falling in love with Morgan would be so dangerously easy, Catriona realised, wandering into her garden to gather daffodils.

She mustn't let it happen.

Loving him would be foolish and hopeless. It could end only in her being hurt all over again.

And more than anything in the world, Catriona feared the pain of losing love. That awful, aching agony of having her heart broken and being suddenly alone.

Catriona was still in her garden when she heard a tremendous commotion from the house, and Eliza came racing through the gateway towards her.

'Come quick, miss! It's the master!'

The two young women ran from the walled garden and into Pelham.

'A couple of carters fetched him home, miss!' Eliza was explaining breathlessly. 'Said they found him by the side of the road. They reckoned he'd been thrown from his horse!'

'So drunk he fell off, more like!' Julian's scathing remark came as he followed the women into the drawing-room.

However, Catriona heard her cousin's sharp intake of breath as he saw his father looking whiter than death, lying motionless on the couch with Hannah agitatedly attending to him.

'Eliza,' Catriona said, turning to the maid, 'ask Morgan to go and fetch Doctor Liddle at once.'

She moved toward her cousin saying, 'Julian, it's cold in here. Get a fire started while Hannah and I make your father comfortable.'

'What?' He stared at her blankly, before nodding absently. 'Er … yes… Of course.'

When Archibald Liddle arrived, Catriona waited with Julian outside the drawing-room while the physician made his examination.

Both Catriona and Julian started to their feet as the drawing-room door opened and Doctor Liddle came grim-faced out into the hall.

'I've warned Samuel again and again that liquor would be the death of him,' the physician said tersely. 'Therefore I sincerely hope he regards this a salutary lesson to mend his ways.'

'So he'll be all right?' Julian exhaled a heavy breath.

'This time, yes. But he's a sick man, Julian. Your father was likely lying out on that road twelve or more hours. He's feverish and weak as a baby, and in need of constant nursing until I say different.'

'Hannah and I will take care of him, Doctor Liddle,' Catriona said.

The physician gave a long-suffering nod and took his hat from the stand. 'When your uncle awakens, you may inform him that if those carters hadn't discovered him when they did, he wouldn't have needed a doctor. He would have needed an undertaker!'

Hannah and Catriona shared the tasks of nursing Samuel Espley. Improvement in his condition was slow, and Samuel was a difficult and demanding patient. He wanted brandy and tobacco, and became foul-tempered and abusive when these were denied him.

One sticky, stifling day when Samuel was being particularly truculent and Hannah was at turns bullying and cajoling to placate him while Catriona coped in the kitchen, Julian breezed through with the nonchalant swagger of one who hasn't a care in the world.

Debonairly outfitted and freshly barbered, he held out a watermarked, silk neckerchief to Catriona.

'Can't get the blasted thing right. Tie it for me, won't you?'

'I'm busy, and my hands are floury,' Catriona remarked shortly, turning back to her bread-making.

Julian had not lifted a finger to help during his father's illness, and the brief moment of vulnerability he'd displayed had quickly vanished into his customary arrogance.

'Eliza!' Julian beckoned the maid, offering the neckerchief. 'A job for you!'

'There!' Eliza tied the knot with satisfaction. 'Very handsome, sir.'

'Many thanks, Eliza. It is indeed refreshing to see a face that is not as sour as cheap wine.' He directed a sardonic glance to Catriona.

'What ails you, cousin?'

'You might make yourself useful here. Goodness knows, with your father the way he is, there's plenty to be done,' Catriona returned irritably. 'Instead of gadding around the country!'

'Gadding?' Julian repeated. 'I have important business to attend to!'

'I can guess where – and with whom!'

'Then you'd be wrong, cousin!' he replied smoothly. 'As well as calling in at the offices of Espley Shipping, I also have an engagement with Maud's father. Not at Larks Grange, I may add – but in his city chambers. I fancy he seeks my advice upon capturing the smugglers.'

'If that is the purpose of your appointment, then I sincerely hope you can assist the judge,' Catriona replied soberly. 'Those fiends are not the noble benefactors they're oft made out to be.'

That night, it took almost three hours for Catriona and Hannah to persuade Samuel Espley to drink his medicine and settle down. When at last he slept, Hannah rolled her eyes to the heavens.

'Praise be!' she muttered. 'You get up to bed, miss. I'll sit with the master.'

'Are you sure?' Catriona queried, glancing doubtfully at her uncle. 'What if he awakens again?'

'I'll likely hit him over the head with summat heavy.'

'That sounds a sterling idea.' Catriona smiled. 'Good-night, Hannah – call me if need be.'

The night was hot. Catriona wearily wandered to the kitchen in search of a cooling drink, starting when she came upon Julian sitting there in the darkness.

'My goodness!' she gasped. 'I didn't know you were back!'

'Been back for hours,' he commented morosely. 'I've been sitting here in the dark.'

'But not alone,' Catriona said scathingly,

eyeing the decanter of brandy at his elbow.

'Comfort, Catriona,' he answered with a self-pitying sigh. 'For my future is in ruins. My plan to marry Maud Loxwood – resurrect Pelham – save the shipping company. They're all ruined.'

In spite of her disapproval, Catriona was curious.

'Whatever did Judge Loxwood say to you?'

'Well, my dear cousin, rumours have reached the judge's honourable ears of a liaison with a married woman!'

'You astound me, Julian!' Catriona stared at him. 'Your actions brought you to this situation, and you haven't a shred of remorse or regret for the unhappiness you've caused Maud!'

'I shouldn't have expected sympathy from you, Catriona,' Julian remarked, his gaze suddenly focussing astutely upon her.

'The worst thing one person can do to another,' Catriona said earnestly, 'is betray trust.'

'Catriona – you've a tender heart,' he said in a low voice. 'Don't waste it upon that hired hand, show me!'

Catriona impatiently jerked free and started for the door, but reaching for her waist, Julian caught her off-balance and deftly brought her down across his lap.

'Let me go!' Catriona cried indignantly, and, struggling against Julian's embrace, she angrily drew back her hand to strike him.

At once, Julian's strong fingers encircled her wrist, and arching Catriona back against his free arm, his demanding lips sought a response from hers.

Catriona was breathing hard when Julian at last released her from his kiss. Scrambling from his lap, she could still feel the hard pressure of his mouth against her own and her senses were racing. 'You're drunk!' she spat.

'I've been drinking, but not so much I don't know what I'm doing.'

'Then you might do something useful, and sit with your father tonight!' Catriona retorted, smoothing down her dress and trying to regain her lost dignity. 'Hannah would certainly welcome the respite!'

She left him and went to her room. Out of caution, Catriona did not light her candle, for yet again the silhouettes of men filing stealthily along the shore were distinct against the silvery tide, once more out-witting the soldiers and evading justice.

When she lay in her bed, she heard Julian going outdoors for his horse. He had not taken her suggestion to sit with Uncle Samuel, but then Catriona had not expected he would.

## CHAPTER SEVEN

That year there was an Indian Summer, with the hot, dry weather lasting far into September.

Catriona was dressing in her coolest cotton and reached into her drawer for her grandmother's amethyst brooch – it wasn't where Catriona was certain she'd left it!

'Eliza!'

Catriona went to her door, calling the maid as she sauntered along the landing with Julian's shirt.

'Have you seen my brooch?'

'I'm sure I haven't, miss!' Eliza retorted, her eyes darting to Julian emerging from his room. 'Why?'

'I didn't intend snapping at you, Eliza,' she said apologetically. 'I'm worried because it's mislaid. It was the last thing my grandmother gave me.'

'I'll keep my eyes open for it then, miss,'

Eliza answered curtly, squeezing by Julian to get on with her duties.

Catriona thoroughly searched her room, then took out each of her garments and shook them gently, lest the cherished brooch be caught amongst the folds, but all the searching in the world did not show the whereabouts of her beloved brooch.

She had no choice but to hope that it would be found eventually.

Catriona awoke early next morning, looking forward to the day ahead with eager anticipation as Morgan had agreed to take her on a picnic at Beacon Point.

She sang softly as she dressed in a becoming cream muslin, a little sad at not being able to pin the amethyst brooch at the dress's collar.

Tripping lightly into the kitchen, she unexpectedly came upon Eliza pirouetting on a chair.

'Ever so pretty, isn't it?' the maid was saying, swirling a brightly-coloured, gipsy shawl tasselled with gold about her shoulders.

'When he gave it to me, I could've– Oh, sorry, miss!'

Eliza stepped down from the chair, folding the shawl decoratively about her arms.

'I was just showing Hannah my new

shawl,' she said with a pert grin. 'Nice, isn't it?'

'Very,' Catriona replied with a stiff smile, for the loss of her amethyst brooch and Eliza's sudden possession of a new shawl flashed together into her mind.

Catriona was at once ashamed of the ugly suspicion. It was unfair to doubt Eliza's honesty ... but how else could the maid afford even such gaudy finery?

'Present from an admirer, it was,' Eliza volunteered smugly, as though reading Catriona's thoughts.

Catriona thoughtfully tied the ribbons of her straw, sun-bonnet, uncertain whether to believe Eliza's plausible explanation.

She was still deliberating a little later when Morgan came into the kitchen to fetch the luncheon basket and they set off together in the wagon for Beacon Point.

It was late that evening and Catriona was quietly playing the harpsichord, her thoughts still distracted.

Julian hadn't yet returned from a trip to Liverpool, so, with Uncle Samuel out on a jaunt, Eliza gone home, and Hannah visiting her brother over at Sandford, Catriona was on her own in the rambling house.

All in all, Catriona was considerably relieved when she heard Julian's horse.

He came into the room sombre-faced, and said nothing. He simply withdrew a handkerchief from his waistcoat pocket, opened the folds, and laid it down upon the keys of the harpsichord.

'My amethyst brooch!' Catriona exclaimed in delight. 'Oh, Julian. Thank you! Wherever did you find it?'

His reply was brusque. 'For sale, in the window of a Liverpool pawnbroker.'

Catriona was shocked. 'Then Eliza did–'

'Not Eliza,' Julian cut in tersely. 'The pawnbroker bought the brooch yesterday, from a man. A man answering Morgan's description.'

Catriona's eyes were wide and horrified. She shook her head vehemently.

'You're not telling me the truth. Morgan would never–'

'Catriona, face the fact!' Julian demanded in exasperation. 'You've been lonely and unhappy, and you've seen only what you wanted to see in Morgan! What do you actually know about him?'

'Everything!' Catriona protested passionately. 'Morgan's my friend.'

'He's used you. He is using you!' Julian

retorted angrily. 'Morgan stole your brooch and sold it while he was in Liverpool to buy a fancy frippery for his girl!'

'Eliza's not his girl!' Catriona cried in consternation. 'She's not! Oh, once I thought she was, too – but I was wrong. Morgan doesn't even like Eliza very much–'

Julian extended his hand challengingly toward Catriona.

'Come with me now – let us confront him – then you shall discover for yourself whether it is I or Morgan Chappel who plays you false!'

'I will speak to Morgan in the morning,' she said, not quite able to still the tremor in her voice, 'and prove your vile accusations wrong!'

With that, Catriona fled to her room, throwing herself fully-dressed on to the bed in a quandary of confusion and despair.

The air was unbearably hot and oppressive, the rumble of the approaching thunder fusing with insistent pounding of the incoming high tide, drumming through and through Catriona's troubled mind until she felt as though she would soon lose her reason...

'Catriona! Catriona!'

A hand upon her shoulder impatiently shook her awake. She opened swollen eyes, stirring with difficulty from a restless slumber that had been unnaturally deep and heavy.

'Julian?' she mumbled. 'What's–'

'For pity's sake, girl. Come!' Julian half-dragged her from the bed, his face and countenance taut with urgency. 'Come to the beach… Hurry!'

Redbird was waiting, saddled and sweating from already having been ridden hard. Julian mounted swiftly, hauling the still-dazed Catriona up across the saddle in front of him. Kicking the mare into a fast gallop, Julian rode north in the direction of Beacon Point.

The tide was at high water when Julian finally halted Redbird in the dark concealment of the stand of gorse bushes surrounding the small cottage which had been Morgan Chappel's childhood home. Swinging from the saddle, Julian unceremoniously dragged Catriona down beside him.

'The smugglers are at work tonight,' Julian began shortly. 'I realised you would not believe me unless you saw with your own eyes that–'

But Catriona wasn't listening.

Gorse Cottage offered a sweeping vista of sea and shore, and Catriona's attention was fastened upon a torch flaring brightly from a short distance along the coast where there should not have been light, while the higher ground of Beacon Point was a wall of blackness.

Even in that split second, Catriona glimpsed the band of shadowy figures far below on the beach, saw the masts of the Isabella, her sails unfurled and full, the vessel tossed like a toy ship upon the swollen, churning, black water as the storm unleashed its fury, spilling a barrage of cold rain like musket fire.

'They're going to wreck her, Julian!' Catriona yelled. 'We have to light the beacon!'

'It's too late. Too late!' Julian shouted, gripping her arms and holding Catriona back from the smugglers' sight.

'The ship's lost, Catriona. No beacon on earth can save her now!'

The mortal screams of the ship's doomed crew, the wrenching and splintering of mast and timber carried sickeningly through the wrath of the storm. Catriona watched in horror as the mighty vessel heaved and foundered amongst the spume-flecked waves, fighting for her life as she crashed again and again on to the ruthless comb of rocks.

Suddenly, Julian took Catriona forcibly by the waist, throwing her to the sodden ground and crouching down at her side.

'Catriona. Over there–' He pointed toward where the false light had burned.

'Look!'

The torch was but a spitting ember now, and the solitary man carrying it was striding along the darkness of the shore as the smugglers put out into the shallows, hungry for the Isabella's riches.

The man stood stiff and still for a moment, before violently thrusting the torch deep into the wet sand to finally extinguish its terrible light.

But in the dying flame of that wrecker's light, Catriona saw clearly the young man's face.

## CHAPTER EIGHT

'I rode out of the dunes and saw the smugglers on the beach. I saw Morgan Chappel with them,' Julian told her when they were back at Pelham.

He was agitatedly prowling the dimly-lit kitchen, swilling brandy from one of Hannah's tin mugs, rainwater still glistening upon his hair and clothes.

'I fetched you to prove to you that Morgan was not the man you think – if only I had had an inkling of what that fiend was truly about I could have raised Loxwood and the military. I could have stopped him!'

'Those poor, poor sailors,' Catriona whispered brokenly, her face buried into her hands as she sat hunched into the chimney corner.

Her head jerked up as she heard the bang of the stable door. Morgan had returned!

'So, he's come back to lie low and play the innocent, has he?' Julian remarked bitterly. 'And not more than a pace or two ahead of the soldiers, I'll wager. Hark at their pistol fire!'

Catriona did not dare to speak his name, for Julian's smouldering anger against Morgan and against all they had witnessed was close to erupting, and Catriona feared what her cousin might do if antagonised.

Despite having seen Morgan there on the beach, despite the most damning evidence of his wrong-doing being before her own eyes, Catriona could not believe Morgan capable of such wickedness. She clung desperately to the hope that there was an explanation, that somehow Morgan was innocent.

'Well, a hasty awakening is in store for the

noble Mister Chappell!' Julian was saying tersely. 'For when Loxwood and the military come asking their usual questions – they shall have him!'

'No!' Catriona's retort was an anguished yelp. 'We must at least hear what Morgan has to say. We can't just assume he's guilty and give him up to the soldiers–'

'Catriona!' Julian exploded in disgust. 'How can you still protect him?'

'I trust Morgan!' Catriona cried despairingly, tearing the admission from deep within her heart.

'I love him, Julian!'

He stared at her, and the atmosphere was charged with an unbearable tension as Catriona waited to know what Julian intended to do.

The silence was split by voices, the clatter of hoofs on the cobbles outside.

'They're here!'

'Julian.' Catriona ran to him, gripping his arm fiercely. 'Don't tell them about Morgan. Let me talk to him first!'

Without a word, Julian strode into the yard to greet Judge Loxwood and the Captain of the Command. The red and white of the soldiers' uniforms were stark against the soft purple dawn, but the men looked defeated and worn, their sweat-streaked horses tired and muddied.

Catriona crept out to Julian's side, her beseeching eyes never leaving his face.

She was not able to take in Judge Loxwood's terse enquiries, listening with growing relief only to Julian's non-committal replies.

'Thank you, Julian,' she muttered shakily, when the military party were turning to leave. 'Thank you for not giving him away!'

'I did it only for you, Catriona. Shielding a murderer does not make me proud of myself!' Julian returned savagely. 'You have one hour with your lover... Then I ride to Larks Grange with the truth!'

Catriona sped for the stables, then froze where she stood, shrinking back into the shadows of the archway.

The stable door was edging open, and Eliza cautiously peeped out, evidently wishing to ensure nobody was about.

Eliza emerged, her pale hair mussed, her clothes disarrayed. Sauntering towards the house, she was fastening her bodice, straightening her skirt, arranging the brightly-coloured shawl about her shoulders.

Catriona's cry of despair was silent.

Past images flooded into Catriona's overwrought mind... Eliza and Morgan laughing together... The two of them going up to the hayloft the night Morgan was hurt... The lost brooch... Eliza showing off her new shawl... Morgan on the beach with a wreckers' light!

Suddenly Catriona's passionate loyalty snapped. The bitter pain of betrayal engulfed her, bringing in its wake a surge of hot, vengeful anger.

Spinning from the archway, Catriona ran through the blackthorns and down the curving drive, her heart hammering.

'Sir!' she shouted, halting the soldiers as they were passing from Pelham's tall iron gates.

'Judge Loxwood. Wait!'

In the nights following Morgan's arrest, Catriona could not close her eyes without seeing again Morgan's face, upturned to the window where Catriona was watching, his eyes meeting hers even as the soldiers dragged him from the stable. Led him bound and captive on the long march to Liverpool and the Castle Hill jail.

She felt no remorse. Catriona's heart had hardened against Morgan. Still notions of Morgan and Eliza together tormented Catriona.

Although neither she nor Morgan had ever declared their love for each other, it had been implicit in every look, every word, in the very closeness they shared. Yet all the while Morgan had been deceiving her. Furtively meeting Eliza. Secretly loving her.

Almost a week went by after Morgan's arrest, and Catriona finally came to realise she would never know a second's peace of mind until she confronted Morgan with the anger and pain his betrayal had brought her.

When Julian was about to leave for the Espley Shipping Office, Catriona decided to accompany him into Liverpool. She dressed in her smart, grey, linen suit and went downstairs. Julian was in the kitchen where Eliza was brushing his coat.

The maid had shown no emotion concerning Morgan's arrest, and Catriona had deliberately taken to avoiding the girl. It was almost unbearable seeing Eliza, knowing she was partner to Morgan's unfaithfulness.

'I deserve it!' Eliza was saying crossly, her pale cheeks flushed by work and annoyance. 'You promised I'd be housekeeper at Pelham!'

'So you will. One day,' Julian replied carelessly, standing while she helped him on with his coat. 'Have you brought down my hat... Catriona!'

He caught sight of her from the corner of his eye.

'Don't stand there hovering, cousin. My word, you look very attractive today!'

'May I drive into Liverpool with you, Julian?' she asked clearly. 'I wish to go to Castle Hill and see Morgan Chappel.'

'I shall be delighted to drive you, cousin,' Julian said, bowing with a flourish and offering her his arm. 'Though, what you want to see him for, I don't know.'

When they arrived in Liverpool, they turned into a wide, steep street.

'Castle Hill is about a mile ahead,' Julian told her. 'A jail is hardly the place for a woman. Perhaps I ought to accompany you inside?'

'I intend seeing Morgan alone,' Catriona replied firmly.

'As you wish.' Julian shrugged. 'However we may have need for subterfuge to gain your entry.'

Catriona looked disconcerted. 'Surely if I obtain permission from the commander of the garrison–'

'Ah, there's a much easier way to do almost everything – if you use the correct influence!' Julian grinned wryly, driving up before the iron-studded gates of the mighty garrison. 'Every man has his price...'

Within minutes, Julian emerged from the watch tower.

'It's arranged, cousin. You may see Morgan,' he said. 'I shall be spending the day at the office. Since we no longer have a hired hand, can you drive yourself home?'

'Of course,' she answered shortly. 'Morgan taught me.'

'I'm sure he taught you well.' Julian laughed softly, extending his arms to help Catriona down from the carriage. 'And much more besides!'

'You really are loathsome!' Catriona returned with disgust.

'Perhaps, but I now realise I owe Morgan Chappel my deepest gratitude,' Julian began slyly, lifting Catriona to the ground, his hands staying about her slender waist as he considered her.

'Nurtured by his attentions, you've blossomed into quite a beauty, Catriona!'

She pulled away contemptuously, and walked purposefully towards the gate of Castle Hill.

Catriona was led across a courtyard where a squad of troops was being drilled, and into the garrison itself.

Catriona shuddered. Her palms were cold and clammy, and she was finding breathing difficult in the close, fetid air.

There were whispering voices, cries, groans and shouts from countless prisoners held beyond the thick, stone walls, but Catriona could think only of one man, and that it was she who had condemned him to this hell.

Presently the turnkey unlocked a door and swung it open, jamming a torch into a bracket just within the cell.

'There you go, miss. Now you can see what you're about.' He stood aside for Catriona to enter.

'This lot haven't the strength to give you any trouble, but I'll be outside if you should need me.'

Catriona nearly cried out in panic when the turnkey slammed the door, and she heard the lock snap home, imprisoning her in the cell.

There was no light other than the guttering torch, and it was several moments before she was able to see.

Her eyes scanned the filthy, emaciated faces of a score of men shackled hand and foot, crammed together in the small, square cell. Too weak even to sit, the prisoners lay in vile straw, staring at her with vacant eyes.

'Morgan!' His name escaped Catriona's throat like a cry of pain.

She ran down the steps and to him, her arms embracing him. Fettered and weakened as he was, Morgan found strength enough to push Catriona aside.

His penetrating, blue eyes were brilliant and blazing with anger as he glared down at her.

'Why have you come, Catriona?' he demanded in a harsh voice. 'Do you gloat to see me so humiliated?'

'Morgan … I'm so…' Catriona stumbled wretchedly, unable to meet his gaze. Unable even to look at him.

Morgan's skin was streaked with dirt, pocked with sores. His thick, black hair filthy and matted. Half-naked, the proud man Catriona had unwillingly fallen in love with was now degraded, stripped of every shred of dignity.

'Go away, Catriona.' Morgan said bitterly. 'For God's sake – go!'

Catriona could not stem the tears that flooded to her eyes. Turning blindly, she almost fell up the steps, rapping on the door for the turnkey to open it.

Catriona was beyond the cell, starting

along the passage, when Morgan's yell of anguish railed after her.

'Catriona. Why did you betray me?'

Catriona drove recklessly down the hill and along the waterfront to the offices of Espley shipping.

She burst past the clerk and into Julian's chambers.

'Oh, Julian. I've done a terrible thing to Morgan!' she cried breathlessly, her face and neck flushed and perspiring.

'He isn't a wrecker. He isn't, oh, he isn't. Don't ask me to explain or prove it, I can't. But I have faith in Morgan. In my heart I know he couldn't be guilty!'

'A pretty speech, cousin,' Julian remarked from his desk. 'However, it's for a jury to decide.'

'No.' Catriona shook her head vehemently. 'I gave Morgan up to the authorities not because of what we saw on the beach, but because I saw Eliza coming from the stables and I realised all you'd said about the two of them being lovers was true.'

Julian surveyed her curiously. 'And you no longer believe that to be so?'

'I no longer care!' Catriona cried. 'All I care about is having Morgan released from injustice! Julian, I need your help! What can I do? Should I go to Judge Loxwood? Or the Captain of the Command?'

'Won't do an iota of good,' Julian said, pouring a glass of dry, Spanish wine. 'Morgan has to stand trial, and there's an end to it.'

'No, no,' Catriona moaned in despair. 'It's my fault he's in prison. I have to get him out.

'Julian, you have influence. Power. You know people,' she began eagerly. 'Couldn't you plead for Morgan, have the charges against him dropped?'

'Not possible. However–' His eyes were never for a moment leaving Catriona's flushed face as she waited in a passion of anticipation for his response.

'Perhaps I could grease a few palms and have him, shall we say, set free.'

'Do it!' Catriona cried ardently. 'Do it now. Straight away!'

'If I were to do this for you, Catriona, I'd be taking a colossal risk. Suppose my part in the plot were discovered? I'd be facing jail myself! Why should I put my life in jeopardy, cousin?' Julian rose, advancing towards Catriona slowly and deliberately. 'What would I gain from this pact?' He smiled at her wryly.

'What will you do to make the danger worth my while?'

'Anything, Julian,' Catriona murmured without hesitation. 'I'll do anything.'

'Anything?' Julian repeated, as though savouring the word upon his tongue. 'That's an enticing offer, cousin. We shall talk of it later.'

## CHAPTER NINE

Catriona was relieved to leave Julian and the teeming city far behind as she drove home to the fresh fields and open sands of Pelham.

It was late afternoon when she entered Pelham's kitchen, having decided to tell Eliza of her visit to Castle Hill. She felt it wisest not to say too much, but for Morgan's sake, Catriona could at least give the maid hope.

'Where is Eliza?'

'Gone, miss,' Hannah returned grimly.

'Gone home already?' Catriona enquired in surprise. The maid seldom left Pelham before eight o'clock in the evening. 'Or do you mean she's gone on an errand?'

'I mean she's gone for good, miss,' Hannah said tersely, banging the copper on to the hob. 'Master sent her packing soon as he got back from being out.'

'Why has she been dismissed, Hannah?'

'I wasn't told and I didn't ask.' The house-keeper pursed her lips.

'Is my uncle in the drawing-room?'

'Master went out again, miss,' Hannah replied. 'But I wouldn't worry myself about Eliza, if I was you. She'll land on her feet all right. Her sort always do!'

Catriona had several hours to compose her thoughts before Julian arrived home to Pelham and they went to dinner together.

During dinner, Catriona was only too aware that Julian was watching her, toying with her, keeping her waiting to learn what conditions she must fulfil to honour her side of their pact.

At last, Julian poured his brandy, lit a cigar, and sat back from the table, gazing across at her with undisguised pleasure.

'To business, cousin,' he began, drawing on his cigar. 'Morgan Chappel will duly go free.'

'When?' Catriona breathed, her intense relief and joy obvious.

'The twenty fourth.'

'That's weeks away!' she protested in alarm.

'It is,' Julian agreed indifferently. 'However, you don't imagine such convoluted plans can be arranged in haste, do you?'

'I suppose not,' Catriona conceded, her eyes scanning his face earnestly. 'But it is definite, Julian? Morgan will be set free?'

'He'll go free.' Julian nodded. 'Now for our pact, cousin. My conditions are threefold.

'When Morgan Chappel is out of jail, you will neither see him nor seek to contact him. Morgan is never to return to Pelham, or to Friars Quay. And finally, Catriona—' Julian paused, obviously relishing the sudden power that he held over her. 'I want you for my wife!'

Catriona was aghast. 'You wish me to marry you?'

Julian threw back his head and laughed at her. 'Cousin. You are shocked by my honourable proposal, because it is to be dishonourable!'

Catriona shook her head, her thoughts spinning. 'I just don't understand,' she commented flatly.

'You regard me a cold-blooded devil, don't you?' Julian enquired wryly. 'I am capable of having feelings, you know! I care for you, Catriona. I admire your strength, and the passionate fire of your spirit.'

Yet you have broken me! Catriona thought bitterly. You are taking everything and leaving me with nothing of my own!

'My inheritance!' Catriona exclaimed suddenly, her plethora of questions at once answered. 'When I come of age and gain my inheritance, as my husband you will control my legacy!'

Catriona leaned across the white-clothed table towards Julian, her clear gaze challenging him to attempt a denial.

'Would you be so ardent to wed with me if I were to be permanently penniless, Julian?'

'Of course not,' he replied shortly. 'Due to my father's – mishandling – of certain events, marrying a wealthy wife is the only way in which I can ensure the futures of both Pelham and the shipping company.

'However, would you be marrying me–' Julian grinned, turning Catriona's question around upon her. '–for any reason other than to save your Morgan's worthless skin?'

Some time later, despite the clear coldness of the morning, Huddy Unsworth's cheeks were scarlet and shining. It was November 25, and the lad was busily occupied shovelling the year's first snowfall from the yard of the coaching inn. Catriona stood watching him pile the snow.

The lad stopped as a military detail cantered into the yard. The sergeant dismounted and strode into the inn to speak with the keeper, while the boy soldier accompanying him scurried to post printed notices upon the inn wall, the door of the smithy, and continued down the road tacking notices at intervals on to the trunks of the bare trees.

Huddy immediately sped to the inn wall, scrutinising the notice, Toby barking and jumping excitedly around the lad's feet.

'It's Morgan, miss!' Huddy yelped, his eyes round and wide.

Catriona was already at the boy's side, her knees weak with foreboding.

'It says Morgan has escaped from Castle Hill, Huddy,' Catriona explained with a sinking heart. 'There's a reward of two hundred guineas been posted for his capture. Alive or – or–'

'A reward out for Morgan!' Huddy echoed in awe. 'Two hundred guineas. Somebody's bound to turn him in for that, aren't–

'Miss?' He looked around in astonishment. Catriona was running from the icy yard out on to the road.

'Miss. Aren't you waiting for the mail?'

'Tomorrow, Huddy!' Catriona replied over

her shoulder. 'I'll come again tomorrow.'

Catriona had not brought the wagon, lest its wheels become bogged into the deep snow drifts, so she hitched her skirts clear of her ankles and leaving the road, started across country towards Pelham.

Julian was shaving when Catriona crashed into his room. Her blood boiling.

'What devious, devilish thing have you done, Julian?' Catriona charged. 'Morgan's escaped from jail. You told me he was to go free yesterday, but he's escaped! Morgan's a fugitive! There are wanted notices everywhere – a bounty for his capture.'

'Steady on, cousin,' Julian remarked smoothly, studying his reflection in the glass. 'You ought not burst into a man's bedroom when he's shaving. Any other time would be perfectly fine, but–'

'Don't you dare patronise me, Julian!' Catriona exploded. 'We had a pact.'

'I told you Morgan would go free.' Julian glanced around at her, all humour gone from his expression. 'He's free.'

'He's an escaped convict. A wanted man!'

'And whose fault is it that Morgan Chappel is a convict at all?' Julian goaded. 'Remember, sweet cousin, it was your testimony which first set the soldiers upon

121

him! Got him out of Castle Hill by the only means possible. And much palm-greasing it took to do it!'

Catriona could not dispute the biting truth of Julian's comments. 'He'll be captured, Julian,' she murmured disconsolately. 'For two hundred guineas–'

'Most folk would betray their own mother,' Julian put in amiably. 'That's true. However, by now, Morgan Chappel is many miles from Friars Quay.'

'Morgan's safe?' Catriona asked, her eyes alight with fearful hope. 'Are you absolutely certain?'

'Morgan went directly from Castle Hill to the harbour,' Julian replied smugly. 'Within one hour of his escape, he was sailing on the tide aboard a Dutch vessel bound for France. Believe me, Catriona, he is far from these shores!'

He laughed shortly. 'You really ought to thank me humbly and be exceedingly grateful!'

Catriona was grateful for Morgan's safety. She was also incensed that Julian had played her every bit as adroitly as a pawn in one of his chess games!

Julian had manipulated her – and Morgan – so both were inextricably caught in the web he had set for them.

'You're very clever, Julian,' she commented tersely, staring past him through the window. 'But don't assume I'm a complete fool. I see through your conniving scheme! If Morgan had been released from jail, he would be a free man. Free to return to Friars Quay and to Pelham. Despite the pact you and I have made. However this way, the way you have arranged it...'

Julian spun around, his face dark with rage. 'You're to be my wife. Never for a moment forget that, Catriona!' He reached out, caught her wrist within his hand, pulling her roughly against him.

'I have your promise and I intend holding you to every word – now you won't even be tempted to seek out your lover, will you, sweet cousin? And as for Morgan Chappel himself. He'll never come back.' Julian's mocking voice was harsh.

'Morgan understands well that all there is awaiting him in Friars Quay is the hangman's rope!'

So winter passed to spring, and spring became summer, and folk in Friars Quay forgot to watch every shadow and stranger lest it be Morgan Chappel.

The wanted notices faded and were tattered by wind and rain, blown away and lost from sight and mind.

Only Catriona remembered. Her first thoughts upon waking, her last before sleeping, were for Morgan.

Knowing he was lost to her for ever blunted Catriona's senses, so she felt little, even at the prospect of her impending union with Julian.

She would be eighteen in a few months, and Julian had informed her they were to be married before the year's end.

Catriona had long ago resigned to the situation. Determinedly suppressing every notion of self-pity or despair, she resolved to make the best of her marriage, and set to building as fruitful a life as possible.

She was coming from the cottage beside the forge, having visited the smithy's wife who was poorly, when Huddy Unsworth raced across from the coaching inn, bursting with news.

'I've found out about Eliza, miss!' he blurted excitedly. 'On market day, it was! I heard some wifies talking. Eliza's gone to the Mawdsley Workhouse!

'The wifies were saying how she'd got herself into trouble, miss.' Huddy frowned, scrubbing his chin with the back of his hand. 'Only I don't know what sort of trouble they meant.'

But Catriona guessed – Eliza was with child… Morgan's! Oh, no…

Catriona lost no time in sending a message to the officers of Mawdsley, advising them that she would visit the workhouse during the following afternoon.

She told no-one at Pelham of her intention to see Eliza, and slipping cautiously from the stable, drove the few miles inland to Mawdsley.

None of the stories Catriona had heard about the parish workhouse prepared her for the brutal reality of the institution. It was far worse than she could ever have imagined.

For all the jealousies and hostilities of the past, Catriona was glad she'd come to Mawdsley. She couldn't allow Eliza to remain in such an iniquitous place, nor for Morgan's child to begin life here.

Catriona sat in the warden's room, waiting while Eliza was brought to her.

Once alone, there was silence.

Eliza glowered belligerently at Catriona from lowered eyes.

'If you'll permit me, Eliza,' Catriona ventured tentatively, 'I should like to help you.

And your child.'

Eliza gave a bored shrug. 'Bairn's been taken.'

Catriona's heart froze. 'Taken?' she repeated fearfully.

'Oh, not dead. If that's what you're thinking, miss,' Eliza returned. 'Taken by a rich couple who likely can't have a lad of their own.'

Catriona's breath caught in her throat. Morgan had a son! But oh, a son he would never see, or know, or love!

'I reckon there's always takers for healthy, baby boys,' Eliza was saying. She met Catriona's eyes defiantly. 'Fine boy, he was, miss.'

'I'm sure he was,' Catriona murmured wretchedly. 'If only I'd known. I could've helped.'

'Why ever would you want to do that, miss?' Eliza mocked, her hard voice edged with contempt. 'You're to wed Mister Julian, aren't you?' she went on insolently.

'And I suppose you fancy he loves you – well, he doesn't! But he'll marry you for the same reason he'd have wed that old maid daughter of Judge Loxwood's!'

'Eliza,' Catriona begged quietly. 'I don't want–'

'I don't give a fig for what you want. You'll

126

hear me out!' Eliza spat venomously. 'I'm not your skivvy any more, I can say what I like and tell you summat I bet you don't know!'

Eliza's eyes narrowed spitefully. 'The only reason Master asked you to Pelham was 'cause you're coming into money when you're twenty one! Master knows what Mister Julian's like, and he reckoned if summat went wrong and Maud Loxwood didn't marry Julian, then he'd fix up a match between the two of you. And that's the only reason Julian wants to wed with you, miss!'

Catriona wasn't at all taken aback by this revelation. Although, it did surprise her slightly that her drunkard uncle had plotted so prudently and with such aforethought.

'Eliza, I want to offer you your old position at Pelham,' Catriona said quietly. 'Will you come back?'

'You want me back?' Eliza queried warily. 'Even after what I just said to you, about Mister Julian and all? And what you know I've done?'

'I came to terms a long while ago with the fact that Morgan Chappel loved you,' Catriona answered softly. 'Yesterday I discovered you'd borne his child.'

Eliza gave her a hard look, and chewed her lip thoughtfully.

'I only wish I had found out sooner,' Catriona concluded sadly. 'When you might have brought your son with you to Pelham.'

'Can't never go back to living in Friars Quay, miss,' Eliza answered after a minute. 'I'd be shunned in the village. No lodgings would have me.'

'Then you need not set foot in the village,' Catriona replied decisively, rising from her seat. 'You may live-in at Pelham...'

## CHAPTER TEN

Now, years later, Catriona stood at her bedroom window, staring out across the shore fields and the cold, grey ocean.

Her wedding day had come. By this night, she would be Julian's wedded wife.

And yet – Morgan Chappel was back!

She'd betrayed him, destroyed him. Why, oh why, was he risking his life to return?

Catriona spun around as her door swung open and Eliza hurried in, her pinched face paper-white and scared.

'I've just seen Mister Julian off to Liverpool,' she said agitatedly. 'But Morgan, miss.

What are you going to do about Morgan?'

'Morgan is a fugitive, Eliza,' Catriona said urgently, taking her cloak from its peg and hurriedly pulling it about her. 'He'll hang if he's captured. I have to find him.'

'Miss, don't say anything to him about me!' Eliza implored, clasping Catriona's arm desperately. 'Or the bairn.'

'Don't you want to see Morgan?' Catriona said, perplexed by the maid's panic. 'Don't you still love him?'

'I don't give a fig for him, miss!' Eliza retorted shrilly. 'And I'd be best suited if I never set eyes on him again for as long as I live!'

'Whatever you wish,' Catriona agreed, her thoughts racing as she quit the room and clattered down the staircase with Eliza at her heels.

'You saw Morgan near the boathouse,' Catriona said hurriedly, turning to Eliza before leaving the house. 'I'm going to find him and talk to him – but tell no-one about this, Eliza. Not Hannah or my uncle, nor Judge Loxwood and the military if they should call asking questions. And especially not Julian. I don't want him to know a thing.'

A dark, brooding figure standing at the water's edge, he was gazing far out across the flat, shifting water. With a pang, Catriona realised this was almost the exact place she had sighted Morgan that fateful night when Isabella was wrecked.

Catriona halted in her tracks at the edge of the dunes. Morgan's back was turned to her, he was unaware of her approach. Now that so few yards stood between them, Catriona was unsure what to do, what she would say to this man she had so treacherously betrayed.

As though sensing her presence, Morgan glanced around. With a cry wrung straight from her heart, Catriona ran to him. Morgan caught her fiercely up into his arms, his midnight-blue eyes deeper than oceans and dark with the intensity of his longing for her.

Catriona raised her face to his, breathing his name over and over.

'This is the first time I've held you,' he whispered brokenly. 'But, Catriona, I've loved you...'

Morgan's words faded as he smoothed Catriona's tousled, blonde hair away from her face. 'You're crying!'

'I expected you to hate me,' she murmured through glittering tears. 'I betrayed you and–'

Morgan's fingertips upon her lips tenderly

silenced Catriona. 'You told what you saw, nothing more.'

'I was jealous, that's the reason I told the soldiers,' Catriona confessed remorsefully. 'I never believed you guilty of wrecking!'

'Then you were the only one!' Morgan remarked bitterly. 'My presence there was damning! You once asked me why I stayed at Pelham... The reasons I gave were true – but there was one other reason also. Long ago, I swore to some day clear my father's name and bring the Espleys to justice. To do that, I needed to be at Pelham.'

'I don't understand.' Catriona shook her head impatiently. 'How are my uncle and cousin connected with your father's being wrongfully imprisoned?'

Morgan's face became grave. He reluctantly released her from his arms. 'So much has had to be unspoken between us for so long, Catriona,' he began regretfully. 'And now we are finally together. Well, there are other things which must be said. Time may be short. You have to know the truth – although I pray I could spare you the pain some of it will bring.'

Catriona swallowed hard, slipping her arm through Morgan's and clasping his hand tightly.

'I've long suspected Julian of leading the Friars Quay smugglers,' Morgan began after a moment. 'That night, I'd followed him from Pelham to the beach. He disappeared into Spinney and I lost sight of him–'

'He'd seen you!' Catriona put in. 'For he came all the way back to Pelham to fetch me!'

'Julian's actions usually do have a shrewd logic behind them,' Morgan commented grimly. 'By the time I gave up searching Spinney for him and returned to the beach, the wreckers' light was burning and the Isabella was already on the Combs. Julian had succeeded in averting suspicion from himself, and damning me, in a single swoop!'

Morgan put a protective arm about Catriona's shoulders and they started walking along the desolate beach, with only the empty miles of sea and sand, the grassy crop of Gorse Cottage, and the high, rugged land of Beacon Point before them.

When he spoke again, Morgan's voice was indescribably gentle.

'Catriona, the Isabella is not the first ship the Espleys have wrecked.'

Catriona stared up at him with growing horror as she absorbed the full, terrible, implication of Morgan's words.

'Oh, no, no,' she whispered miserably. 'Not the Rhiannon.'

Morgan drew her closer, so Catriona's cold cheek was resting against his chest.

'The Rhiannon was Samuel Espley's ship,' Morgan began carefully. 'She was to bring a shipment of gold ingots from New York to Liverpool. The gold was never put aboard. The crates contained only bars of worthless pig iron. Samuel Espley had devised an elaborate embezzlement, not only to steal the gold, but to swindle his insurers, too. He placed amongst Rhiannon's crew a band of hand-picked men. When the Rhiannon was far out to sea, these men were to mutiny. Take the ship off her course, and scuttle her in waters where her wreck would never be discovered. The mutineers were to escape aboard a sister vessel, which would be lying by, and sail on to Jamaica.'

'So, my uncle would secretly have possession of the gold, while claiming its loss from his insurers?' Catriona ventured fearfully. 'And for the loss of the Rhiannon also... For which your father, as her captain, would be deemed responsible?'

'That was the Espleys' plan. And near foolproof it was too. Except that my father uncovered the plot to mutiny and foiled it.

Mutiny is a capital offence, and when the perpetrators were cornered, they lost no time in naming Samuel Espley as author of the scheme. Obviously, Pa wrote a full report into the Rhiannon's log, and he confided the details to your father, whose honour he respected.'

'Your father and mine knew each other?' Catriona queried in surprise.

'They'd sailed together often and were friends,' Morgan replied with a reflective smile. 'It's strange to think of their knowing each other, isn't it? Being friends, all those years ago?'

Catriona nodded sorrowfully, and Morgan held her even closer as they climbed the windswept dunes.

'The Rhiannon proceeded along her true course,' he continued after a moment. 'When she was sighted safe and sound approaching Liverpool, Samuel and Julian were forced to take desperate measures. Once the Rhiannon docked, their part in the embezzlement and mutiny would be revealed. They had to ensure she never reached harbour,' Morgan murmured, touching his lips tenderly to Catriona's throbbing temple. 'They lured the Rhiannon on to the rocks with a false light.

'I was here, just below Gorse Cottage,

watching my father bring his ship home–' he added quietly. 'I saw Samuel and Julian down on the beach with their wreckers' lantern.'

'They murdered my parents!' Catriona cried in great distress. 'Why are they both free – why weren't they arrested and punished?'

'Proof, Catriona! There isn't a shred of proof,' Morgan answered bitterly. 'Only the word of a disgraced ship's captain, and the witness of his eleven year old son!'

'The ship's log!' Catriona almost shouted. 'What of the report your father entered? That's proof, isn't it?'

'Pa was depending upon the Rhiannon's log being retrieved from the wreck and exonerating him,' Morgan said tersely. 'Even the crates containing the bars of pig iron would have been proof enough to clear his name. But Samuel and Julian left nothing to chance. They were close in those days, as thick as thieves. Before official divers arrived to make their search, the Espleys rowed in the dead of night out above the wreck and dived upon her, setting explosive charges.

'They destroyed her completely,' Morgan concluded, his anger surfacing. 'When the official divers went down a few days later, all they found of the Rhiannon was a flotsam of driftwood!'

'So the Espleys got away with murder,' Catriona exclaimed harshly. 'By simply blowing up the evidence!'

Morgan's jaw set stubbornly. 'They gutted the wreck all right, and Samuel Espley was injured in the process – but not before he had searched for and found the ship's log!'

'Are you sure?' Catriona demanded quickly.

'No. However, I believe that log book is the reason your Aunt Amanda left Pelham and never returned!'

'Amanda knew?'

'Not in the beginning, not for years. I'm sure of that. Amanda took me in after my mother died, and made me one of the family,' Morgan added briskly.

'One night, Amanda and Samuel went to a ball with the Loxwoods at Larks Grange. I always enjoyed seeing all the finery and the carriages and suchlike. Pelham was splendid then, with a full staff of grooms and servants. So, I stayed awake to wait for them coming home.

'I watched from the landing. Amanda looked beautiful as always in her French gown and jewels, but Samuel was rather drunk, and had to be helped to bed by his valet.

'So Amanda was left to return her jewels to the drawing-room safe, a task she never did herself, since Samuel always insisted upon opening and closing the safe personally.'

Morgan's eyes were burning with conviction.

'I'm convinced Amanda found the log book. Or some other evidence that incriminated her husband and son in the Rhiannon's wrecking, for the very next morning she left Pelham and took your cousin Lucy with her.'

'If you're right, then Amanda can testify—'

'If Amanda didn't go to the authorities then, she won't now,' Morgan replied quietly. 'Perhaps she was unable to go on living in the same house as Samuel and Julian. But she couldn't send her husband and son to the gallows either!'

'Do you suppose the log book still exists?' Catriona asked eagerly, the germ of an idea in her mind. 'Do you?'

Morgan shrugged. 'After Amanda left, I never was able to get into the drawing-room, much less tackle opening the safe!'

'I could try!' Catriona cried fervently. 'I

could slip in and–'

'Absolutely not!' Morgan returned. 'I wouldn't have told you any of this, had I thought you'd respond in a foolhardy way! Make no mistake, Catriona – if you cross the Espleys, your life will be at risk!'

'Finding the log book is the only chance of ending this!' Catriona retorted.

'No, don't even attempt to search, Catriona!' Morgan forbade. 'There is another possibility of getting to the truth.

'After escaping from Castle Hill, I was put aboard a Dutch brig bound for France. I jumped ship at Land's End, and I've been scouring the ports for the few sailors who survived the Rhiannon's wrecking.'

'Of course. There were other survivors!' Catriona exclaimed, adding doubtfully. 'But weren't they questioned at the time?'

'They were. And either they didn't know anything, or were too intimated by Samuel Espley's power to speak against him,' Morgan admitted.

'However, that's years ago and I thought perhaps now...' He shrugged. 'Fear lasts a long time, Catriona. I've found only one of Rhiannon's sailors, a sick old man who is still too afraid to bear witness against the Espleys. But there are other survivors, and

I'll find them,' Morgan concluded decisively.

Catriona reached up to sadly, tentatively, touch Morgan's mouth with her lips. 'You're in peril every moment you're here in Friars Quay,' she murmured. 'Why have you come back?'

'I had to,' he answered shortly. 'When I learned of your betrothal, I had to come! Don't you understand, Catriona,' Morgan said vehemently. 'I can't bear even the notion of your being Julian's wife!'

Catriona broke free of the sweet temptation of Morgan's nearness. 'Go away, Morgan. Please, please, go away,' she begged, desperate in her fears for his life. 'Don't you see it's too late,' Catriona murmured truthfully. 'Nothing can stop the marriage now!'

Downcast and deeply troubled by her anxieties for Morgan, Catriona's heart sank in dismay when she stole through the November dusk into Pelham's yard and saw Redbird cropping the tough grass outside the stables.

Julian was already home from Liverpool.

The kitchen door opened, spilling light across the cobbles. Eliza darted out to meet Catriona.

'Did you see Morgan, miss?' she queried

agitatedly. 'Where is he?'

'I'm not sure,' Catriona replied despondently. 'Gone, I pray.'

Catriona and Eliza went together up into the house. Even from the kitchen, Catriona could hear the irate, raised voices of Julian and his father rowing behind the closed doors of the drawing room.

'Did Julian miss me?' she enquired indifferently.

'Huh! Too busy going at it hammer and tongs with the Master!' Eliza retorted. 'Just hark at 'em!'

For once, Catriona actually welcomed the animosity between the Espleys!

'The Master's already had a drop or twenty,' Eliza went on scornfully. 'By the wedding, he'll be proper drunk. Mind, there's nowt queer 'bout that, eh, miss?'

Catriona gave a resigned sigh, and sank wearily into the chimney corner.

Hunching her knees up close against her chest, Catriona closed her eyes, burying her face into her folded arms exactly as when she was a small, dejected child.

But she wasn't a child. Catriona was a woman, and the responses the touch of Morgan Chappel's hands and lips had awakened still ached unfulfilled deep within her.

'You love him, don't you, miss?' Eliza blurted out. 'Morgan, I mean?'

'Yes.' Catriona half-smiled, her answer barely a whisper. 'I believe I always have and always will.'

'Thought as much.' Eliza chewed her lips, deliberating. 'You've been good to me, miss, fetching me from the workhouse and all. I owe you summat for that.'

'You don't owe me, Eliza.' Catriona shook her head. 'Not a thing.'

'Begging your pardon, miss, but I reckon I do. And that I ought to tell you summat.' Eliza began, glancing around to make certain Hannah was still occupied in the pantry and well out of ear shot.

'It's about Morgan and me…'

## CHAPTER ELEVEN

'That night, miss – the night the Isabella got wrecked – Mister Julian turned up at my lodgings in the village,' Eliza began hesitantly. 'He had a plan, you see, to get rid of Morgan.' The maid avoided Catriona's eyes.

'Julian said he'd make me housekeeper if I

141

did exactly like he told me.'

Catriona caught her breath. 'Which was what, Eliza?'

'I had to come to Pelham and make sure nobody saw me,' the maid answered in a low voice. 'After Morgan got back from the beach and went up to bed in the hayloft, I was to hide in the stables and wait. When Julian gave the signal, I was to hang on a minute or two, then sneak out of the stables and make it look like I'd – like, well, you know, miss.

'But it wasn't that way at all!' Eliza cried, her voice rising shrilly. 'Morgan Chappel didn't even know I was in the stables! There wasn't ever anything happened between me and Morgan–' she concluded vehemently. 'Not that night, nor never!'

Catriona stared at Eliza blankly, not quite knowing what to make of the maid's outburst. 'But what of your child?' she asked after a pause.

'It wasn't his, miss.' Eliza looked away uncomfortably, her words dropping so low that Catriona could barely hear them. 'My bairn is Mister Julian's.'

Catriona's full attention snapped back upon the maid. 'Does Julian know?'

'I should say he does!' Eliza retorted

scathingly. 'Why do you reckon he had the Master dismiss me from Pelham!'

'The deceitful, selfish, heartless...!' Catriona bit her lip. 'How could he condemn you and his own flesh and blood to that – that – vile, godforsaken institution!'

'Out of sight, out of mind, I reckon, miss.' Eliza shrugged matter-of-factly. 'It was–

'Tea's still hot, miss!' she interrupted brightly, as the kitchen door opened. 'Sure you won't have a cup?'

'Tea? There's no time for tea parties, girl!' Julian remarked, striding into the kitchen and bending to kiss Catriona's forehead.

'Shouldn't you be making ready? We'll be leaving within the hour!'

'I shall be ready,' Catriona replied stiffly, rising from the chimney corner. 'Eliza will assist me.'

'I will, miss!' Eliza bobbed a curtsey and scurried past Julian into the hall.

Catriona moved by Julian, his hand across her hips arresting her in mid-step.

'I'm eagerly anticipating our union, Catriona,' he murmured against her ear. 'Unfortunately the old man insists upon accompanying us to church. However, since he's embarking upon a gambling and supping jag directly after, we shall be free to relish the first hours of our marriage alone.'

'Excuse me, Julian,' Catriona said crisply. 'I have to change.'

Once within Catriona's room, Eliza hurriedly shut the door fast and spun round to Catriona, her thin face animated and aghast.

'You're never still going to wed him, miss?' she exclaimed in consternation. 'You can't be!'

'Oh, but I am,' Catriona replied evenly.

The prospect of marrying Julian was now more appalling, more repugnant to Catriona than ever before. Yet becoming irrevocably wedded to Julian was surely the only means Catriona possessed of deterring Morgan Chappel from ever again returning to Friars Quay.

Catriona turned calmly to the maid. 'Eliza … please fetch my dress.'

The November night was cold, and Catriona's empty heart colder still as she drove with Julian to her wedding.

The carriage wheels crunched through frost lying thick upon the rough ground, and the rising moon was near to full, blurred with a gauzy halo. Its chill light spilled stark upon white fingers of water frozen into stillness along the roadside ditches.

Throughout the drive, Catriona scanned the dark landscape for any glimpse of Morgan Chappel. She had the uncanny, fearful sense that Morgan was near, and her only emotion at reaching the small, Norman church was intense relief that her ominous presentiment was wrong – and Morgan had not appeared.

Going up the church steps, Catriona glanced over her shoulder into the bleak, winter night. Perhaps Morgan was long gone from Friars Quay after all…

The church was lit only by a solitary branch of candles. Shadows clung to the corners and alcoves, the altar was bare of flowers, the rows of dark pews empty.

Samuel slumped to seated close to the aisle, and taking Catriona's hand, Julian led her to the altar.

'Enough of your cantish babble, Burwick!' Julian said presently, irritably interrupting the minister as he began to read from the book of prayers.

'Get on with it, can't you–'

'There'll be no marriage this night – nor any other!'

The soft voice had uncanny resonance as it echoed up to the heights of the stone church.

Morgan!

Catriona stood absolutely still at the altar, not daring to even glance behind. However, in that fleeting instant, regardless of her fears, Catriona's heart sang!

Morgan was here – somehow, in some way, they would be together! Catriona would be his, and his alone!

'Morgan Chappel!' Julian's face twisted into an ugly sneer. 'So, even a bounty of two hundred guineas upon your life could not keep you away from your little playmate!'

'You're not going to marry Catriona,' Morgan announced calmly, stepping from the shadows of the rear alcove. 'You're a murderer and a wrecker, Julian, just like your father!'

Samuel Espley suddenly lurched to his feet, rounding upon his son. 'Damn you, Julian!' He swayed drunkenly, falling back into the pew. 'Damn you to eternal hell! Didn't I tell you? But you were so clever!' Espley spat derisively. 'You had to twist the knife, get your revenge…'

Neither Morgan nor Julian paid any attention to Samuel Espley, their total concentration was focussed upon each other, and upon Catriona who stood between them.

Morgan started along behind the rear

pews towards the aisle, and Catriona felt Julian's hold about her tighten.

'I shall presently delight upon delivering you to Loxwood and claiming the two hundred guineas paid for your corpse, Morgan,' Julian jibed, and now Catriona sensed his swift, almost imperceptible movement.

Simultaneously, she glimpsed the dull gleam of candlelight upon gun metal as Julian withdrew a sidearm, levelling the small pistol at Morgan Chapel's heart.

'Meanwhile,' Julian continued smoothly, 'the marriage proceeds!'

Reverend Burwick nervously licked a dry tongue over his lips.

'No,' he said at last, steadfastly closing the prayer book. 'I'm not a brave man, Mister Espley, but I'll not condone your profanity of the Lord's holy place, nor hear your vows of matrimony!'

Julian threw Burwick a scornful glare as the minister hastened to quit the church, while the pistol's aim remained steadily upon Morgan Chappel.

'You shall pay for this with your life, Morgan,' Julian commented, looking his adversary square in the face. 'I'm calling you!'

Catriona saw an unexpected smile play wryly upon Morgan's lips.

'So, you fear what I may now have to tell Loxwood,' he queried. 'And seek to silence me by exacting the Espleys' own brand of justice!'

'Choose your weapons,' Julian challenged. 'If you have steel and stomach enough for the encounter!'

'Pistols.' Morgan's rejoinder was terse.

'So be it.' Julian pushed Catriona ahead of him as they started back up the aisle.

Morgan stood away, leaving their path clear. However as they drew level, Catriona twisted free from Julian.

'I'm not going back with you!'

'You'll do as I tell you,' Julian remarked indifferently. 'You're still a minor, and my father is your guardian. Which effectively means,' he carelessly indicated Espley's staggering from the church, 'that I am your guardian, Catriona. And your only living relative.'

Julian's gaze snapped to Morgan, and Catriona could not comprehend the intelligence which transferred between them.

'Do not entertain the notion of spiriting my cousin from Pelham by stealth of this night, Morgan,' Julian continued urbanely. 'I shall shoot you down as a trespasser, and as for Catriona ... I admit to wanting the girl for my wife – but if anything unfortunate were to befall her.' His lips curled into a cruel smile. 'Catriona would be worth just as much to me!'

'Neither your greed nor your threats intimidate me!' Catriona protested untruthfully. 'I shan't go with you!'

'Go, Catriona!' Morgan ordered bitterly. 'Return to Pelham – and make no attempt to leave!'

'Your playmate guides you wisely, sweet cousin,' Julian remarked, ushering her from the church.

He paused on the steps, donning his hat and tugging its brim in mock salute to Morgan Chappel.

'I look forward to our meeting upon Beacon Point…'

Neither Catriona nor Julian uttered a single word during the drive out to Pelham. However, when they were inside the house, and Catriona was about to go up to her room, she allowed herself to beg an explanation to that which had troubled her since leaving the church.

'Julian, why are you and Morgan to meet at Beacon Point?'

'Oh, cousin! You don't understand, do you?' He laughed harshly, taking her hand

and pressing it to his lips. 'At sunrise, we are to duel!'

Catriona sedately climbed the stairs, but once away from Julian's view, she fled along the landing into her bedroom, firmly turning the key in the lock lest Julian, in the brutality of his present mood, should seek to enter.

For all her resolute determination of past months, Catriona now felt as helpless and vulnerable, as hopelessly trapped as she had in her earliest days with the Espleys.

Catriona steeled her nerves, summoning every ounce of inner strength to suppress the panic-stricken, fearful emotions surging inside her. She fastened her thoughts upon the imminent duel – and the need to somehow prevent it.

What could she do?

Forcing herself to act methodically, Catriona lit her lamp, changed from the wedding dress into her sturdy, everyday clothes, and sat beside the window, her fingers anxiously knotted into her lap as she racked her mind for a solution.

Despite her promise to Morgan, Catriona finally realised what she must do.

Moving from the window to her bed, Catriona lay down. Far too tense to sleep, she stared up at the ceiling, listening for Julian to retire.

It was long past midnight before she heard his footfalls upon the landing. He paused outside her room, and Catriona blessed the lock that would hold the door fast if needed. However, Julian did not try to enter, his footsteps continuing on along the landing.

Catriona crept to the door. There was no time to lose. Inching open the door, she cautiously peered out on to the landing.

Julian had passed beyond his own master bedroom, and was letting himself into Eliza's box-room, hungry for familiar comforts.

Catriona waited only a second longer before stealing downstairs.

Once in Samuel Espley's drawing-room, she lit her lamp and made for the safe.

She realised immediately that it would store nothing of value, for the locking device was broken. The safe swung freely open, and Catriona quickly rifled through the dog-eared bundles of worthless papers inside.

She stood, hands pressed to her hips.

Which other secure hidey-hole was there? Where would Samuel Espley secrete something as dangerously valuable as the Rhiannon's log book...?

Catriona slipped off her shoes, speeding

up the stairs again.

Julian would no longer entrust such incriminating evidence to his father's safe-keeping!

If the log book still existed, then Julian Espley himself would have possession of it!

Inside the master bedroom, Catriona shut the door soundlessly and with hammering heart, scanned the large room. The oak secretary in the fireplace alcove!

Seconds later, the salt-stained, water-blurred log of the brigantine, Rhiannon, was hers!

The drawer contained a sundry of other documents also. Dates, names, places, figures. Julian apparently kept meticulous record of his contrabanding activities.

There was, too, the solid, gold seal of the Isabella. And only one way in which Julian Espley could have obtained it.

Galvanised by the striking of the clock and the few remaining hours before dawn, Catriona quit the master bedroom. Darting into her own room, she retrieved her amethyst brooch for, if her plans ran well, Catriona was keenly aware that after this night, she might never again be beneath Pelham's roofs.

Out from the house, across the yard and into the stables, Catriona patted the mild-mannered grey, speaking softly to the mare, as she passed along the row of stalls to Redbird.

The spirited thoroughbred shifted restlessly as Catriona's cold, trembling fingers fumbled with the numerous buckles and straps of bridle and saddle.

Tossing her head, Redbird responded to Catriona's feather-light touch upon her mouth, and galloped effortlessly for the shore.

Morgan was nowhere in sight, and with night already ebbing, Catriona could not tarry farther.

Heading up amongst the dunes and into Spinney, Catriona rode like the wind for Larks Grange to fetch the judge.

Dawn was close to breaking across the eastern sky as Catriona and Judge Beverell Loxwood made haste towards the beach.

Catriona marvelled that the elderly gentleman had paid any heed to the dishevelled, young woman pounding at his door in the wee small hours.

However, even if Loxwood hadn't comprehended much of Catriona's garbled explanations, the log book and other documents which she placed into his custody made sense enough for the judge to direct a messenger to Castle Hill Garrison, requesting the military to converge with all possible speed upon Beacon Point.

Emerging from the scrub pines and climbing the inland-facing rugged gradient of the Point, Catriona was distraught to sight five men already assembled out on the windswept crest of the high land.

'They've begun!' Judge Loxwood cautioned her in a low voice. 'Be silent, Miss Dunbar. They must have no distraction.'

Catriona stifled her cry of anguish. After all, after everything that had happened, she was too late to stop it.

Morgan and Julian were back to back, pistols raised against their chests. Archibald Liddle's voice carried distinctly on the keen November wind as he counted out the ten paces before the duellists would turn and fire their weapons.

The crack of pistol shot tore the dawn silence.

Catriona looked, saw Morgan half-crouching, spinning around. Julian was standing squarely, already facing Morgan, a thread of acrid smoke curling from the muzzle of his raised and discharged pistol.

All Catriona saw or understood was Morgan – alive and safe!

154

'Thank heavens!' she breathed. 'It's over!'

'It's far from over, Miss Dunbar.' Judge Loxwood's authoritative tone bludgeoned Catriona's euphoria.

'Your cousin's fired prematurely, dishonourably,' the judge added in disgust. 'Julian Espley is a coward!'

'I care nothing for what he is,' Catriona cried in frustrated exasperation. 'May I now go and tell Morgan the news? That he is exonerated, and his father's name is cleared at last?'

'In a moment, Miss Dunbar. In a moment,' Judge Loxwood replied. 'The duel must run its course. Morgan will aim and fire at his leisure.'

'Morgan won't do that!' Catriona protested incredulously. 'He'd never...'

'He must,' Judge Loxwood cut in shortly. 'Espley is disgraced, his name and family shamed. Unless Espley faces Morgan Chappel's fire, he shall not redeem a shred of honour.'

'The Espleys are beyond shame, Judge Loxwood,' Catriona murmured, her attention fixed upon the grim scene being played to its finale upon the Point. 'Their honour past redemption.'

'Hold your fire, Morgan!' Julian's call was

low and tense. 'What gain is there for your killing me? Every man has his price – and I well know yours!

'The girl.' He grinned confidently. 'Spare my life, and she's yours.'

Morgan remained silent.

'What of your father, Morgan?' Julian persisted. His throat was tight, his face wet with cold sweat. 'He's been in jail a long while. He's getting old, Morgan! May not have much time left. You could get him out, clear his name, with my help!'

Morgan raised the pistol a fraction, keeping its barrel steadily levelled at Julian Espley.

'I've got the Rhiannon's log book, Morgan!' Julian continued, staring transfixed across the yards into the pistol's barrel. 'Iron-clad proof of my father's guilt.'

Morgan still said nothing, but drawing back the hammer of his pistol, he slowly took aim – and discharged the shot harmlessly into the ground.

'My quest was not for vengeance, Julian,' he said tersely, throwing the smoking pistol aside and striding from the Point. 'Only for justice!'

Catriona broke away from Judge Loxwood, flying to Morgan. Unable even to speak, Catriona buried her face into his chest, holding Morgan to her as though she would never let him go.

She was scarcely aware of the red-coated soldiers galloping over the rise, fanning out and swiftly closing in to arrest Julian as he lunged for Redbird and made one final, frantic bid for escape.

'Miss Dunbar, Mister Chappel!' Judge Loxwood cleared his throat, approaching the couple briskly. 'The Captain of the Command advises me that within the last hour the body of Samuel Espley has been discovered in Briarley Brook. It is uncertain,' the judge concluded solemnly, 'whether Espley suffered an accident and drowned – or deliberately took his own life...'

Later that morning, when pale, winter sun gleamed upon the lapping, slate-grey waves of the incoming tide, Catriona and Morgan wandered together upon the wild, desolate shore.

Pausing at the old boathouse, Morgan drew Catriona nearer. She responded instinctively. Moving against him, wanting to hear his every breath, wanting to feel the beat of his heart so close to hers.

'Will you marry me, Catriona?' he murmured, stroking the softness of her hair.

'Will you?'

Catriona met Morgan's blue eyes, her fingertips tenderly exploring every contour of his face and mouth.

When she touched her lips to his own, the warmth of Catriona's kiss offered Morgan every answer he desired...

This Large Print Book, for people
who cannot read normal print,
is published under the auspices of

## THE ULVERSCROFT FOUNDATION

... we hope you have enjoyed this book.
Please think for a moment about those
who have worse eyesight than you ...
and are unable to even read or enjoy
Large Print without great difficulty.

You can help them by sending a
donation, large or small, to:

**The Ulverscroft Foundation,
1, The Green, Bradgate Road,
Anstey, Leicestershire, LE7 7FU,
England.**
or request a copy of our brochure for
more details.

The Foundation will use all donations
to assist those people who are visually
impaired and need special attention
with medical research, diagnosis
and treatment.

Thank you very much for your help.